I0545598

DEEP EDGE

Harrisburg Railers, book 3

———————————————

RJ SCOTT

V.L. LOCEY

Love Lane Books Limited

Copyright

Deep Edge (Harrisburg Railers #3)

Copyright © 2017 RJ Scott, Copyright © 2017 V.L. Locey

Cover design by Meredith Russell, Edited by Sue Laybourn

Published by Love Lane Books Limited

ISBN - 9781785646201

All Rights Reserved

Dedication

To Rj – To all the women who discover a new dream or career later in life and chase it despite the naysayers. Dreams can change and come true after fifty. You're never too old. Go for it! ~ V.L. Locey

To Vicki – for wonder twins, Zucc, and our Olympic figure skater. And always for my family ~ RJ Scott

With grateful thanks to Meredith Russell for her beautiful cover. Rebecca Hill for her editing and for making us look good. Rachel Maybury for sorting us out. And to our army of proofers for their hard work.

DEEP *Edge*

— HARRISBURG RAILERS 3 —

RJ SCOTT &
V.L. LOCEY

Love Lane Books

ONE

Trent

I studied the image of me at the Sochi games. I looked so happy with that silver medal around my neck, standing just a few inches lower than Connor O'Day, my teammate who'd grabbed the gold. Even though Connor – the bitch – had won the gold, I'd still been happy. I recalled that feeling. Happy was nice.

"Trent?"

Two silvers in the past two Olympics. The upcoming one had been supposed to be mine. I'd been skating stronger than I ever had. Everyone had predicted that I'd finally get past Connor to win the gold. Happy would have been everywhere. I'd have been *drowning* in fucking happy. I would have been wearing happy and that gold around my neck like a cashmere coat from Neiman Marcus.

"Trent?"

Gayle's touch pulled me from Envy Land. I spun from the newly hung imagery of Trent Hanson on the soft white walls of my new agent's office. She smiled sadly at me. Gods. Everyone looked at me like that now. I hated it. And I hated not being happy anymore.

"Sorry, I was just admiring that costume. Isn't that dark blue and silver to die for?" I moved around the short, dark-haired woman who was now in charge of my career. Or what was left of it.

"It is. It still amazes me that you design all your skating costumes. You're such a talented young man. Why don't we sit, and we'll get to the reason I called you in?"

Ah, agents. They were so lovely – when they weren't embezzling all your money and spending it on whores, vodka gimlets, and a particularly bad run over a week in Atlantic City. Note to the young and innocent – never let your stepfather manage your money, especially when he's open about how much he dislikes your gay little ass. That way you won't end up broke, shamed, and trying to figure out how to keep your mother and grandmother from being booted out of their house while your rink teeters on the edge of financial ruin. Where the *fuck* had all my happy gone? I wanted it back, dammit!

I moved past the windows that looked down on Philadelphia, my hometown. I'd been born and raised in the City of Brotherly Love. I adored this city, and it loved me in return. Or had. Now I was just the mincing and well-dressed queer who didn't even have two pennies to rub together. How quickly love and adoration turned to titters and cold shoulders. Drawing my coat around me, I sat down in a plush beige chair and crossed one leg over the other, making sure my coat draped properly over my thighs. I hate wrinkles. And beige. Why were straights so afraid of a little color?

Gayle sat down behind her desk, smiled at me yet again, and folded her hands in front of her. I raised a freshly plucked eyebrow. She was still trying to get a handle on me. Tobey & Troy was the largest athletic repre-sentation firm in Philly. They handled most of the Eagles,

Sixers and Flyers, as well as several tennis players. And now they had me. Trent Lawrence Hanson. Famed gay figure skater and next in line to be a Dickens character in real life. Please, sir, I want some more. Ugh. As if I'd eat gruel. What if I had to? The thought was too much to bear.

"I think that now that the legal issues with your father—"

"Stepfather," I quickly reminded her.

"Yes, sorry, stepfather. Well, now that he's been convicted and is serving time, I think this is the moment to start working on marketing you in a positive light." She smiled again, nervously, and leveled light blue eyes at me. "Where are you in terms of returning to competitive skating?"

I glanced out the window at Ben Franklin standing atop City Hall. I began running my hands over the thin cotton flaps lying over my thighs.

"I have no money, my professional reputation is shot, and both my rink and my mother's house are two months away from foreclosure. Do you honestly think I could find the mental clarity and focus to skate again?" As soon as I heard how bitchy I sounded, I placed a hand over my mouth. "I'm so sorry," I mumbled into my fingers.

"It's quite understandable," she replied. She was far too nice to be saddled with a miserable cow-bag like me. I wanted to cry, but didn't. I'd do that later when I visited Mom and my *Lola*. "Would you like something to drink?"

"Water would be lovely," I coughed into my fingers. She rang her receptionist. "I'm better now. See." I lowered my hand and smiled brilliantly at her.

Gayle nodded, but melancholy lingered in her gaze. A tiny blonde hurried in with a bottle of water and handed it to me. I was about to ask if she could possibly find a cold one, but I bit my tongue. Bitchy Trent had already escaped once today.

"Thank you."

She nodded and scurried out, closing the door behind her slim backside. Her shoes were terrible. Who wears black flats with a peach dress in late June? Honestly, women, learn how to dress. I took tiny sips of the tepid water. Gayle waited. I capped the bottle and balanced it in my left hand so my coat didn't get watermarked. I was a beggar now. I had to keep my wardrobe in good shape. Tears threatened again.

Gayle broke into the building weep-fest. "I understand that you're not mentally ready to return to figure skating. To that end, we need to find you something to do that will bring in good money so you can get your assets back in sound fiscal shape."

"You mean pull my rink and my mother's house out of the snapping jaws of foreclosure?"

"Well, I wouldn't have been quite that dramatic…"

"Few are." I sighed as I returned to working out the crinkles in my duster.

"Right, well, I've been approached by GLBTQtv about a reality show with you as the star."

My chin dropped to my chest. "Get. Out."

"I'm very serious," Gayle said, her smile spreading into a grin. "They're waving a nice fat contract at us."

"I'll do it! Wait. Are there lots of zeros mentioned in the contract?" I was so excited I grabbed my duster and wadded it up in my right hand.

"There are several zeros," she whispered as her grin grew even wider.

"I'll do it!" My gods, I was such a whore. Wave a ten in front of me and down to my knees I went. But zeros meant money. Money that would keep my family safely housed and my rink operational. Rainbow Skate was *my* rink. I'd bought it and refurbished it. It was where I practiced. And it was where little gay and straight children who wanted a safe place to skate and express themselves and their art could come. No hateful slurs or brutes were allowed at Rainbow Skate. That was my rule. I hated bullies. I'd dealt with them from the time I was eight and discovered how fabulous I was on skates and how amazing my sewing skills were. By the time I was fourteen and came out officially, not one person was shocked. My stepfather was disgusted, but then again, he was a thieving twat.

"Wonderful! I've read over the contract and it's pretty straightforward." I bounced in my seat as Gayle talked. "They're asking for six to eight weeks with exclusive access to you and the Railers as you work with them."

The bouncing slowed. "I'm sorry..." I tapped my right ear. "Did you say Railers? What are Railers?"

"They're the hockey team that's expressed a pointed interest in working with you on this show."

I couldn't control the laugh that burst out of me. I roared so long and so heartily that I was close to hyperventilating when the laughter began to die down. Gayle sat behind her desk, staring at me as if I'd gone around the bend.

"*Phew.* Oh, my gods and garters," I panted several minutes later. Dabbing gently under my eyes, I saw a blur of black on my fingertip. "And I thought this was waterproof eyeliner. Do you have tissues?"

She got up , grabbed a box from the edge of her desk, and handed it to me.

"Thank you." I wiped my finger on a Kleenex, then gingerly pulled a tiny corner under my right and then left eye. "I hate this cheap stuff. I'm going to throw it out when

I get home. Why did I even buy anything other than waterproof?"

"Is there a problem with you working with hockey players?" Gayle asked after she sat back down.

I tittered. "How much time do you have?" I asked.

She gawked at me.

"I do not do jocks."

"But you're a jock."

"Uh, no, no, I am not. I'm an artist. I don't go skating around hitting people in the face with sticks. No, sorry, this sweet thing," I motioned to myself, "does not do hockey players, footballers, baseballers, basketballers, or those men who run around with nets to catch balls in. Lacrosse! I don't do them either. I *will* do tennis players or an occasional fellow skater, but they can't be on my team. Cat fights amongst team members are so ugly. I rather like Russian skaters. It's the accent. I once did a Russian skater. He was delicious. I called it my Boris Godunov phase."

I giggled at the witty, but Gayle simply continued to gape. I was so happy now – why was she being a prude?

"What?" I asked when she didn't speak.

"Trent, this contract is contingent on you working with the Railers."

"No, sorry. I don't *do* hockey players. Didn't we just cover that? They're rude bullies who have never passed up an opportunity to shove me into lockers, dunk my head into toilets, or taunt me in front of everyone at the rink. Nope. Tell them I don't do hockey players."

"Trent, the contract is very specific. The Railers recently had a player come out."

I passed the water bottle from my left to my right hand. "Good for him. I wish him all the success in the world. This impacts me how?"

"He and his coach…"

"Ew. His coach? Oh, yuck. Have you seen coaches? Ugh. They're usually old Russian men with nose hair and breath that always reeks of potato soup and pickles."

"Trent, what the man looks like isn't important…"

"Maybe not to you."

"They're hoping to have this gay player and his teammates spend a few weeks with you at Rainbow Skate. It will show the world that gay athletes are caring, competitive, normal people."

"If the nematodes out there in TV land don't know that we're normal people, then fuck them in the ass with a splintery wooden spoon. Again, I state that I do not do hockey players."

"Then the show goes to Connor, since he's recently come out as questioning."

I shot to my boots. "There is no way in *hell* I get beat out by that simpleton again. How *dare* he try to out-gay me?! Gods above, I *hate* that little shithead. Fine. *Fine*! Tell the TV people I'll work with the Cro-Magnons on skates, but the first time I hear one homophobic remark or one of them corners me in the bathroom, I am out of there!"

I slammed the water bottle on her desk and stalked to the door, my duster snapping around my leather ankle boots.

"Before you go, you need to read and sign the contract," Gayle called, stopping my perfect diva exit cold.

I glowered at the door, turned, and walked with purpose back to my seat. I snapped the contract from her and flopped down. Oh my. There were so many zeros. I needed zeros so, so badly. Why was nothing easy? Hockey players. I shuddered, read, and signed.

"I feel so cheap and dirty," I mumbled ten minutes later when I was standing on Broad Street. I tied my coat around my waist. Some fool walked past and asked if I knew what fucking month it was. "Yes, I know it's June. The outfit needed a coat. Don't judge me."

I hailed a cab. I don't drive cars unless I must. I do have a scooter, but it had looked like rain when I left.

"2020 South 16th Street," I told the driver after I was in and seated. He flipped the meter on and off we went to my mother's house.

I was torn now. On one hand, I was the happiest I had been since my stepfather had run off with all my money. On the other hand, working with big, dumb hockey players was going to be dreadful, even if one of them *was* gay. I spent the ride staring out at the city and the narrow streets.

Newbold – or Point Breeze – was where I'd been raised. There was a nice Asian community there, with plenty of people from Laos, Indonesia, Cambodia, and the Philippines, which was where my *Lola* was from. Mom and my grandmother had been trying to keep their heads above water since the debacle with my stepfather. The taxes were overdue on her little brick rowhouse. I'd paid them for years, but now…now I didn't have the cash to pay my own rent. Then there was the mortgage on Rainbow Skate.

"My life sucks," I groaned when we pulled up in front of my mother's place. There was no way the cab could get to the curb. Cars were parked bumper to bumper.

"Welcome to life, kid."

"I'm twenty-three," I told Mr. Cabbie. He shrugged. Someone behind us blew their horn. The driver gave them the finger. I paid, and tipped the best I could. I felt the dark look for the measly buck tip as I hurried out of the yellow cab and up the cement steps to blessed relief from the nasty old world.

Lola was in the kitchen when I blew in. She gave me one look and opened her arms. I ran to the short, round, silver-haired woman and pulled her close. She stroked my back and murmured to me in Pilipino. The room smelled of soy sauce. Maybe she was making chicken adobo. I really needed some of her cooking, but I needed her hugs more.

"Where's Mom?" I asked during the embrace.

"At the shop," *Lola* whispered.

I grimaced, then gently stepped away. "I thought she had today off," I sighed, peeling my coat off and draping it just so over the back of the battered chair. I sat down and quickly had a platter of dark chicken thigh meat cooked in soy, garlic and vinegar served over rice in front of me. "She works too hard."

"Not more or less than any day since he run off with money."

I blew out a breath and forked up some rice. Mom needed rehab. But, again, rehab cost money.

"I got an offer to be on a TV show. They want me to star in it with hockey players," I told my grandmother.

She stopped waddling around long enough to point to the bright orange shirt she was wearing. "You make TV with Flyers?!" She pointed at the logo on her boobs.

"No, not the Flyers."

"Pah, then bad hockey team."

"They're from Harrisburg."

"Almost as bad as Pittsburgh!"

Lola loved her Flyers. As did everyone in the city except me. I didn't do hockey players. Ever. Except now it looked like I was. Curse my stepfather to hell and back.

"They're going to pay me a lot of money to do the show, *Lola*. We need the money. I can pay off the house and the rink. I can help Mom financially so she's not giving mani-pedis for dismal pay and tips seven days a week."

She sat down across from me at the table that was as old and worn as she was. Hell, as the whole *house* was.

"You are good, sweet boy. Eat more." She patted my hand.

Try maintaining a skating weight with two Pilipino women in your life. It's almost impossible. But, since I'd probably never skate again, why not have more rice? Who cared? It wasn't like one of the Railers would be looking at the delightful curvature of my ass. Shit, it had been ages since anyone had looked, commented on, or even patted the delightful curvature of my ass.

"May I have more rice?"

TWO

Dieter
———————

I can't recall the last time I felt like this.

On top of the fucking world.

My agent Bob Stiller was next to me, pen in hand and papers in his lap, negotiating the next part of my slow-moving career. Stiller had been my agent since I was seventeen, and he'd done well by me so far. In fact, I was just coming to the end of a two-way contract with most of my time spent at the Carlisle Rush, the AHL development team that fed the Railers NHL time. It wasn't my dream to get stuck in the AHL with the chance of playing with the big boys just out of reach but it was steady money and I was *so close* to making it big.

I'd actually spent the end of the season with the Railers, covering for injuries, and I'd even played in a few of the playoff games before they were booted out in round two.

Me, playing for the chance of winning it all. My name on the Stanley Cup. After all this time.

We hadn't made it far, but hell, the Railers were a new

team and they hadn't been expected to get to the playoffs, let alone get past round one.

But I'd been part of them getting there. Done well. Great, actually – with one goal and five assists over the ten games, I'd made a name for myself; the press said the Railers should contract me full time, talked numbers in the millions. I was the undrafted grinder who'd worked himself into a team, and I was fucking proud of myself.

"So, how have you been?" asked Dawson Brown, the Railers Manager, steepling his hands and tapping his chin. The familiar stance was one Brown used when he was thinking about serious things. Like whether or not I deserved to keep playing for the Railers. "Carlisle Rush speaks highly of you."

"Thank you, sir. I've loved my time with the Rush." And I had, I wasn't lying. They were good guys. Some of them would never make it any higher, certainly never to the NHL, but they were a solid team and I'd shone there.

I had decent numbers in my role as first line left wing for the Rush – this past year I'd pulled in a solid seven goals and thirty-four assists over the year. I was the team playmaker, and I loved it.

"I won't yank your chain," Brown began, and rested his hands on the table, right over the beige folder that had my name on it. "Our salary cap is tight; it's common knowledge that it cost us big money to get Tennant Rowe up from Dallas. With Hurleigh signed for the next five years and Addison's contract up for negotiation, we're very tight."

"Rowe was a good call," I said when he paused for a moment. Like I needed to interject some kind of observation. Rowe was what some people called a generational player – one of those good enough to carry a team when they needed it.

"At the Railers, we pride ourselves on fair and equitable terms, but not even us can fight the cap only increasing by two million this year, and with you being only one of five restricted free agents we want to keep."

I'll take that, I thought. *I'll take two million. Hell, at this moment I'd take two dollars, because I need some fucking stability.*

And then I realized what he'd said. He'd explicitly stated that I was one of the guys he wanted to keep. Nothing about being sent back down on a two-way contract, my time split between the Rush full time and covering the Railers if they needed me.

"So, when it came to offers, which we have for a few players…"

He fanned out the folders, and I counted five of them. I knew exactly who was in those files, and I'd put myself up against the other four any day. That wasn't bravado or arrogance; that was self-assurance underlined with a small amount of chemically enhanced pride in my achievements. Brown waffled on again, about superiority and standards and the future, and all I could think was, *Cut to the chase already.*

"We'd like to make you a qualifying offer, one year, eight hundred."

I should be over the moon with that – another year with the Railers was exactly what I craved – but I knew better than to say a thing. Stiller would deal with the money.

"We might well look to take that to arbitration," Stiller said. Because he had to – he had to believe as my agent that I was worth more. But what if the Railers turned around and told me to leave; that they didn't want me if I fought?

I wanted Stiller to stop talking. He didn't, but that was his job.

I listened as Stiller asked questions, including arbitration, respect, and lots of other buzzwords that I barely listened to. Being more invested in my future wasn't a financial thing for me – it was the team, and the hockey, and that was mostly it.

"We'll take this away with us," Stiller said, and he stood up, and I copied. He extended his hand to shake Brown's, I copied that as well, and then we were out in the corridor.

We didn't talk until we were out of the East River Arena and down in the parking lot. My practical Toyota was parked up next to his car, and looked the worse for wear against the gleaming silver paintwork of his Beemer.

"How do you think it went?" I asked.

"How do *you* think it went?" he countered.

Great, I hated when people answered questions with more questions.

"Well, I think eight hundred is good money. I know it's only a year, but I can prove myself and we can end this season with a multi-year contract."

He nodded and clutched that folder with my name on it to his chest. "It's a good offer," he said. "I agree it gets you a steady year in one place – no more traveling between here and Carlisle, no more fragmented seasons. I just don't know what to say."

I looked down at my feet, then up at the sky, leaning back on my car. What was he trying to say? "Do you think I'm worth more? That I should fight for more?" I asked, but I didn't really want to hear what he was going to say. The last thing Bob Stiller did was blow smoke up players' asses; he was straight as they came, and you knew he did his best with what he had.

"Yes and no," he hedged, which wasn't like him, and I looked at him, startled. I'd expected an unequivocal yes, because in my head if I was worth the Railers taking me for a year, why would he disagree with that, and what the hell was the no for?

"What do you mean, yes and no?" I had to prompt him, and he stepped closer and lowered his voice.

"Of course you're worth that year with the Railers – you keep your head down, work on your conditioning, get better watching the veterans, get fitter, and you could be looking at a multi-season deal this time next year."

"You know I can do all of that; I'm a hard worker, and my fitness is good."

He looked at me and made that face, the one that meant he wanted to ask me a question but didn't know how to ask it. I steeled myself for the inevitable.

"Yes, it's good, I've seen the numbers…it's just not stellar."

"What?" I thought my numbers were more than just *good*. After all, the Railers were willing to take me. I would be in the NHL, baby. I'd arrived.

"How's everything else?"

"Like what?" I was a master at delaying the inevitable.

He raised a single eyebrow in answer.

"I'm doing good," I lied, using my standard reply.

Bob sighed dramatically, opened his car door, and tossed the file inside. Then he turned back to me, and I knew he was going to say something bad – I could see it in his expression.

"This is the last year I can represent you, the last contract I negotiate on your behalf. I'm not taking this to arbitration. We'll sign off on the eight hundred, and then you need to get another agent."

"What the fuck, Bob—"

"I mean it, kid." He stopped my righteous anger in its steps with his low warning tone. "You need to sort your shit out. I'm putting my neck on the line for you here, and I don't like the way it compromises me. You need to fix yourself, get some help."

"I don't know what you're talking about," I said so fast he winced.

"Jesus, Dieter, you're in fucking denial, but I've seen you. I know you've popped so many fucking pills—"

"Keep your fucking voice down," I growled, and stepped into his space in a classic intimidation move. We didn't know who the hell was standing behind the cars listening to this shit. "I'm clean and you know it."

"You were," he said shrewdly, and stared right at me, daring me to argue.

"I have a legitimate fucking injury from the playoffs," I said, still in a low voice, still right up close to him, using my six-inch difference in height and my weight to intimidate.

"You were doing so well, kid."

Anger speared me. "I'm not a fucking kid."

"I didn't disclose your prior problem to the Railers. Don't make me regret that."

"I don't have a problem," I said. Again, the standard reply, the same one I gave even to myself.

I'd been checked into the boards hard halfway through the final game the Railers had played in the playoffs. It had hurt. My knee hurt. I needed meds to help my body heal. It wasn't like I was back to taking twenty a day. I was responsible.

This time Bob's sigh was more heartfelt. "Jesus," he began, and shook his head. "You're a good kid, Dieter, but I have to take a step aside. You understand that, right? It's nothing personal."

Bob has been with me since day one, and he was going now? Right here in this fucking parking garage, he was telling me he was done? What kind of agent was he to abandon a player who'd just been offered his first real honest-to-god NHL contract?

"Fuck you, Bob," I snapped, because he was an asshole, and I shoved him a little, because hell, I was furious at his betrayal.

Bob shook his head and was in his car and gone a long time before the tension in my chest eased. Who did he think he was?

"Everything okay?" someone asked from behind me, and I turned to face a serious-looking Tennant Rowe, the player with a shiny new multi-million-dollar contract and stupid floppy hair.

He's second line for a reason, second-rate in the NHL, and he only got traded in because of his name. I could be him. I should have been drafted, and I would have if I had brothers who played for the big teams. Fucking asshole Tennant Rowe with his fucking brothers.

I leaned back on my car again, my breath stolen by the corrosive hate that ran through those thoughts. Ten wasn't there because of his family name; he was future first line for sure, probably captain one day – he had a skill and speed that sometimes defied the odds, and he was possibly even a future hall of famer.

Where had all that hate in my head come from?

"D?" Ten asked again, and came to stand in front of me with so much concern on his face that I wanted to punch it off him, stamp him into the floor. There it was again – a violent hate that flowed through me. I bent at the waist and put my hands on my knees.

Ten didn't stop. "Jeez man, was it bad news?"

The grapevine would have informed everyone of who had meetings when, and it was no secret that I was one of the five guys the Railers were looking to take on. Ten was just showing compassion.

"No, I have a year's qualifying contract," I said, still

bent over. "Bad Chinese." That was the only thing I could think of to explain if I looked gray, or wheezy, or bent at the fucking waist like this. I made an effort to stand up straight, slowly, to avoid an inevitable head rush, and came face to face with Ten, who still looked worried.

"Should I call someone?" he asked.

"No, it's cool."

Ten extended his hand, which I took. "Congrats on the contract."

"Thanks, man."

"So I guess they'll ask you about the conditioning thing this summer. It's part of a reality show, getting this ice skater to help us with our speed. I signed up because I really think we could learn something from figure skaters, you know…"

I listened and nodded in all the right places, but mostly what I wanted was a bottle of water. I excused myself, probably mid-sentence from the open-mouthed expression Ten had going on, and I drove out of the garage. Only when I was away from the Arena did I pull over to the curb. The half-finished bottle of water in the car was luke-warm, but it didn't matter, because it washed the pills down, and that was its only purpose.

My knee throbbed and I needed the help.

I sat there for a good five minutes, flexing my fingers on the steering wheel and watching the clock. Placebo effect or not, my muscles began to loosen five minutes in, and I finally drove back to my apartment. Closing the door was like shutting out the world, but there were two messages on my machine. One from Layton Foxx, the expert the Railers had called in to handle the big, gay coming-out of Ten and his boyfriend Jared. He didn't know everything going on with me, but he did know about the sex tape, and he was dealing with the situation.

"…so I think it could be a case of getting out in front of this, Dieter. Give me a call when you're back, and we can talk strategies."

Layton was all about the tactics – how to manage huge, life-changing things in a way that didn't have fans leaving the arena in droves. He rambled on about times and possible dates and something about summer projects for speed and fitness. I stopped listening after a while, like I had done with Ten. I didn't have time to listen to people – I had things in my head that needed organizing.

Marianna's message was far more to the point.

"Twitter say you 'ave new contract. My price is up. Call me."

That was all she said, in her lilting French accent, but the softness in my thoughts filtered it to a meaningless nothing that couldn't worry me. She should release the fucking tape, and maybe I'd get famous off the back of it. I pulled a couple of beers from my fridge and settled on the sofa, watching reruns of an eighties game show, not quite understanding why I was finding it all so freaking funny but loving the happiness that was filtering through my veins.

I had a contract, I felt good, my knee wasn't hurting, and I had a beer in my hand.

God knew where Bob got off saying he wouldn't rep me. There were a hundred agents out there who could make me more than he did. Some of them would spin the hell out of a sex tape so I came out of the shit smelling like daisies, with a legion of fans – both sexes – who would all want a piece of me.

But the longer I lay there, as the gorgeous softness in my thoughts morphed back into that hard place I was used to in my head, the more my brain process stalled on one thing.

How was it that I was happy for the world to see me butt naked in a three-way, fucking some random guy, but I didn't want people to know I wasn't brave enough to deal with pain without meds?

But the answer was easy.

It was easier to admit to sex than to admit I needed pills to keep me sane. No one could ever know.

THE EMAIL that arrived the following morning, with me nursing a hangover and Marianna's message still on my machine, was short and to the point and not all that welcome.

I clung to the fact that my lawyer had demanded we put a restraining order on her after she wouldn't leave me alone. Stalking wasn't the best thing to deal with, but it had been the only thing until the appearance of this fucking video she was holding over my head.

I couldn't think of Marianna now. I had to focus on the team.

An invitation was offered to all team members who hadn't pinned down plans to attend a conditioning and speed camp, and I recalled Layton's message – well, the half of it I'd listened to. He'd said something about a good idea, and all I could think about was team-building, and having something to do with the long summer that stretched in front of me.

I took a couple of the small white pills and let them work their magic before I signed up; my knee ached a bit, and I needed them.

Seemed like I was attending a training camp with some sparkly-assed figure skater, and for the life of me I couldn't think why I was agreeing. I found the Wikipedia page for this Trent Hanson guy, but I didn't really need to look to know who he was. The Railers might be big, bad hockey guys, but ice was ice. I knew who Trent was, had seen him on the news with his medals and his success, recalled something about his manager fucking him over.

"Join the club," I said, and saluted the empty room with my first beer of the day.

And then that familiar warmth filtered into my brain and I lay back on my sofa looking up at the ceiling.

Hiding out at a camp would probably be a good thing right now.

And hell, working with a figure skater was going to be some funny shit.

Just like that time I wore the number 69 on my jersey in college on a dare.

Freaking hilarious.

THREE

Trent
___

We could hear them talking. I peeked around the corner and saw them all gathered in the corridor. Eleven or twelve of them. Thirteen if you counted a leaner man with dark hair who didn't look like be belonged among the troop. A baker's dozen of them waiting for me to arrive so the torment could begin. Why had the week leading up to this gone so quickly? I'd been trying to drag it out, but it had marched on without a care for Trent. Time was a bastard.

I pulled back from the corner and looked right at my agent. Her nose was pink from the cold in the ice rink. I loved her little teal jacket, and made a mental note to ask later about where she'd gotten it.

"Are we sure we don't want Jane Goodall in the leading role of this show?"

Gayle gave me a withering look. She was quickly perfecting that expression. It would serve her well. Damn. I should have worn one of my tiaras just to twist some nipples. Not that what I'd pulled on wouldn't get things rolling as soon as the simians laid eyes on me. Had Trent dressed to stir things up? Oh yes, Trent had. I'd gone with the anime look for the day. Colored and teased hair, lined eyes – which didn't count because I line my eyes daily – skin-tight sapphire leggings under a short, flouncy kilt of green, blue, and white, topped with a tight blue-and-white sweater. Oh, and bright blue hiking boots and a few dozen bangles on each wrist.

"They look like very nice young men," Gayle sagely replied. I rolled my eyes, then peeked at my grandmother. It looked like there was an angry pumpkin at my side. *Lola* was bundled up in a number 17 Flyers sweater over a Flyers hoodie. She had the hood tugged over her silver hair and all one could see were two dark, unhappy eyes. Probably her tiny feet were in Flyers socks.

"What do you think?" I whispered to my grandmother.

"I no like." She folded her arms over her breasts. "They all cheap shots."

"See, *Lola* agrees. Cheap shots." I popped a hip and waved a gloved hand in the general direction of the Railers.

"Cheap shots or not, the contracts have been signed and the camera crew will be here tomorrow. So why don't you go say hello? I'm sure these gentlemen are nothing like the immature boys you went to high school with."

I chanced another peek. That was quite true. The guys in this group were even *bigger* than the teenage players who had made every trip to the rink a gauntlet run. Granted, they were good-looking in that "grunt-fuck" sort of way. Burly, strapping men – aside from the previously mentioned nonconformist – who took up lots of room and air. There was one in particular who seemed even gruntier and fuckier than the others, if that was even possible.

He appeared aloof, standing with the group yet separating himself from it. Tall, shoulders as wide as the boom on a sailboat, waist tapering in from those monstrous shoulders, legs long and thick from his years on ice. The man really had incredible thighs, but then again so did I, although proportionately much smaller. Thank god for blue jeans and men who knew that fitted jeans were the *only* ones to wear. The color of his eyes was a mystery from this distance, but his striking jawline stood out, as did the dark whiskers to match his rumpled hair.

His demeanor was off. The others talked and laughed, but he hung back, hands in his front pockets, eyes on his sneakers. Standoffish and hot. Just toss in at least one major personality flaw and a dislike of men who wore eyeliner like other men wore flannel, and we had the basic recipe for every gorilla who pushes a puck.

"Nope, no. I cannot do this." I said.

The odd man out of the group looked my way and smiled. I jerked my head back and tried to hide behind the scowling pumpkin in lime green Muk Luk boots.

"Dammit! I've been spotted. Shit."

Gayle was about to tell me to stop being such a peri-winkle-toned pussy when the apes rounded the corner, led by their handler or something similar.

"Trent, it's great to finally meet you. Layton Foxx – I'm the Railers' head of social media, and a huge fan. Adler and I caught your show when you were in Harrisburg. I've spoken with your agent over the phone a few times, and we're very happy to have been able to make this happen."

I let him grab my hand and pump it while my eye met and held that of Mr. Aloof. He had pretty but shadowed gray eyes. I watched the way his eyes widened a bit when he saw the eyeliner and the cobalt tint I'd washed into my hair the night before.

"Charmed," I murmured, trying to rip my gaze from

the man lingering at the back of the pod or troop or whatever one called a gathering of stick-wielding apes.

"Let me introduce the guys. They're all excited to be taking part in this."

Mr. Foxx – and yes, he was – led me by the hand to the Railers. They were all so damn tall. I tried not to look at the man in the back, but something about him kept compelling me to peek at him. There was sadness and envy in his eyes when our gazes touched during my introduction to Tennant Rowe, the brave man who had come out about his relationship with his coach, Jared Madsen. Jared, by the way, blew my theory about all coaches being ugly old Russian men with ear hair long enough to braid and decorate with twinkle beads right out of the water. Tennant and Jared made a striking couple, and their affection for each other rode on the cold air like the scent of magnolia on a summer night.

Trent, darling, stop waxing poetic about the gorillas. They look good, sure, but they will throw shit at you like all the other dirty monkeys.

I shook hands with all of them, names like Adler and Arvy all blurring together the closer I got to Mr. Aloof with the soulful eyes. He reached for me before Layton could make the proper introductions. Even with my thin blue gloves on, his touch lit up my skin. The heat of his hand and the strength of it seeped through the sheer cotton material covering my palm. Warmth spread over my fingers and raced up my arm to my face. Or was I just being fanciful? I do that on occasion, according to others.

"Trent, this is Dieter Lehmann. He's just signed a nice one-year contract with the Railers to play left wing."

"How exciting." I glanced back at Gayle. She jerked her head at the man grasping my fingers a little too tightly.

"So, uh, Dieter, what do you think you can learn from me?"

"What can I learn from *you*?" he asked me back. I nodded and prepared for hate comment number one to spew forth. "Speed, using the edge more, learning how to turn more quickly on the ice."

Oh. All of that was true. Shit. And not even a snort of derision. Odd, to say the least.

"And you're comfortable with a prancing little poof of a figure skater being the one in charge?"

"Totally," he replied, and I wasn't quite sure we were still talking about skills on the ice.

"*Trent*," I heard Gayle gasp. Mr. My-Eyes-Could-Be-a-Robert-John-Song continued to stare at me.

"You suck," I heard *Lola* say.

That broke the intensity of Dieter and Trent. My attention went to my dear, sweet grandma poking Tennant Rowe in the chest. The top of her head *maybe* reached the center of his chest.

"Excuse the snippy pumpkin otherwise known as my grandmother," I said loudly, and spun away from Lehmann and his mysterious eyes. "She's not a fan."

"Yeah, I can see where her loyalty is," Rowe replied with a fetching smile. "You have a great team here in Philly, Mrs. Hanson."

"Damn right!" *Lola* boasted, then grinned at the gigantic men smiling down at her.

"Why don't we give the Railers a tour of the rink, and then we'll have lunch at Pat's and talk about what the network is hoping to see from this reality show?" Gayle said like a trained game show hostess, even going so far as to motion gracefully to the ice arena.

The tour was quick and concise, speedily showing the Railers where everything happened. As we lingered along the boards, I explained to those gathered around me what I hoped we could accomplish.

"This rink is my life. My dream." I patted my chest gently. "This rink is a safe zone for LGBT youth who have been bullied, demeaned, and persecuted by friends, family and society. As we all know, toxic masculinity is rampant in sports. I've battled institutionalized homophobia in figure skating for years. Hatred comes down on children early, and it cripples them emotionally and creatively. I'm doing this show to save Rainbow Skate."

I wouldn't discuss my personal reasons, although the world knew I was flat broke. I did have some pride left.

"I think we can do some good, truly I do. Maybe we can show the bigots out there watching that gay athletes and straight athletes aren't all that different. Maybe a scared future skater or Railer will be watching and feel empowered. So while you'll come away with new skills that I'll impart to you, the world at large will also benefit."

"And what are you going to come away from this with?" Dieter asked, his voice rising from the murmurs of agreement from the team, my agent, and my grandmother, who seemed to be getting over her hatred of the Railers. She had been hanging on to Jared Madsen's elbow for the entire tour, filling his ear with talk ranging from hockey to the popularity of ice skating in her homeland to how she felt he was living a deprived life since he'd never had *lumpia*, a kind of meat-filled eggroll enjoyed in the Philippines. A hundred bucks said that when she arrived at the rink the next day, she'd have pans of *lumpia* for the Railers.

"Me?"

Stellar reply, Trent.

"Yeah, you. What are you hoping to learn from us?" Dieter persisted.

"Well, it's certainly *not* going to be fashion sense." I gave them all some shade.

The majority chuckled. Only Dieter didn't. He seemed incredibly intent on me for some reason. It made me feel quirky and nerved up. It was the depth of his scrutiny, I think. Whatever it was about the man, it had me twitchy, not unlike how I felt sitting in the kiss-and-cry area after a performance.

"I'm not sure about anyone else, but my stomach is telling me we're late for lunch. Shall we head for this Pat's?" Mr. Foxx slipped into the awkward moment.

My gaze was still locked with Dieter's until the group turned and headed for the exit. Even as he was walking off, my sight was on his broad back.

What did I hope to learn from this experience? I didn't have a damn clue. Seriously, what could skating baboons teach *me*? It was all about the money for Trent Hanson. I did know, however, that there were a million sad mysteries in Dieter Lehmann's stunning eyes, and I was a curious little creature at heart.

LUNCH at the famed cheesesteak eatery had been akin to watching the hyenas at the Philadelphia Zoo being fed. Do they have hyenas at the zoo? It's been years since I've been. Not important. The Railers ate like starved predators. That's the important imagery. I ducked out of the feeding frenzy early, citing the feeble excuse that my grandmother needed a nap.

Mom was home from work when we arrived. She asked if we'd eaten.

Lola and I had shared a plain cheesesteak, each getting half. I might not be skating, but I did *not* want to creep over one-forty if at all possible. My clothes would be tight and I'd get snippy and ugly. A man of my height – 5'9" – should never be over one-forty and expect to look smashing in spandex competition pants. Also, maybe someday when my money woes were gone, I might want to get back into the game. I still wanted a gold medal. But that was a big maybe.

Focus on the present, Trent. Focus on how that Dieter man ate his food while never taking his eyes off you. He's either hot for that perfect ass of yours or planning how to get you alone in the men's room and dunk your head in a potty.

"I hope he's hot," I mumbled as my mind spun something lurid about me and a – *GASP!* – hockey player.

"You hope it's hot?" My mother asked.

I shook off that horrifying fantasy. Obviously it had been too long since I'd had my dick sucked. Maybe I'd hit the clubs tonight. Philly had oodles of them. It's a proud and vibrant gay community there. But clubbing cost money. Perhaps I should call an old flame? No, they all were mad at me, hence them being *old* flames. Christ. Jerking off was getting old.

"Trent. Did you bring your grandmother's cane in?"

"Sorry, I was thinking about…that snowman from *Frozen.*"

The look was priceless. Mom could toss side-eye as well as a drag queen, which was obviously where I'd learned it from. Her sassy look was lacking, though. The dark bags under her deep brown eyes were telling. They told me I was a failure as a son and a businessman for allowing that bastard who shall not be named to use me in this manner.

"She had it when we came in. Probably she stuck it in the umbrella rack by the front door like she always does."

Mom sighed. She did that a lot concerning my *Lola.* And me too, I was sure.

"Mom, why don't you take tomorrow off? Come to the rink and watch them make a TV show about your son?"

"Trent, baby, I have to work tomorrow. My appointment book is full."

She reached up to pat my face, then returned to whipping up some canned chicken soup for her dinner, since *Lola* and I had pigged out on cheesesteaks well after noon. Mom wasn't much taller than my grandmother, and I wasn't much taller than my mother. A peewee. Ugh. See? Spending all day with walking sequoia trees was making me feel puny and unseen.

"Have one of the other manicurists take them. I'll pay you for the day. Just come to the rink. Please? I want you to be part of the show."

She waved me off with an uncomfortable laugh. "No one wants to look at me. They've seen my stupid face enough over the past year. They want to see you, not this dumb shit who married a man who stole her baby boy's money and spent it on other women, racing dogs and blackjack."

"That is *so* not the case." I wrapped my arms around her and pulled her close. I heard her quivering inhalation. "Mom, we all misjudge people. Look at my ex, Gunther. I thought he was a human being. Turned out he was a carbuncle."

She snorted. "But you didn't marry him."

I kissed her soft black hair. No, I hadn't, but I'd entertained thoughts. Then he'd got tiffy about my travel schedule and the lack of sex and gone out and cheated on me with Alexander Kruglov, my arch nemesis on the Russian figure-skating team. Fucking Gunther. The boil.

"What's past is past. Please, come to the rink."

"Maybe some other day, Trent. I like to work. It keeps

me from thinking about what I did to your life. I should have stayed a widow."

"Mom, you thought you were doing good by finding me a father."

She shoved away from me, her anger palpable. "Some father I found you. He hated everything about you once you started discovering yourself."

"Well, he found one thing about me that he liked. My money."

She frowned at the can of water in her hand.

"I'm sorry. That was unkind of me to say. But Mom, this is not on you. If anything, I should have been more aware of my cash flow. But *no*, as long as I had money for travel, clothes and boy toys, I was happy to be in the dark."

"I miss your father so much."

I knew she did. I'd never known him. He'd been killed in a car accident when I was a baby. I think I missed what I *assumed* a good father would be. I missed the man she'd told me about. A common man who'd worked at a dealership garage fixing imported cars, and loved life. They'd met young, fallen in love, and made me when she was just fifteen. *Lola* had *not* been happy, but the kids had gotten married, so she'd settled down eventually. Dad had been eighteen when he'd died six months after I was born. Mom looked older than she was, which was just a few months shy of her fortieth birthday. Life had been hard for Donna Hanson Gallo. It showed in her eyes and the slump of her slim shoulders.

"He'd be proud of us. We don't give up." I padded over to her and took her hand in mine so we could dump the water into the pan together.

She smiled weakly up at me. "He would be so proud. He always said you had great things ahead of you."

"So sometime you'll come to see the show being taped?"

"Yes, sometime, Trent. Just not tomorrow." She stirred the condensed soup into the water and set the pan on the stove.

I lingered by the old fridge, my attention pulled to the blue gas flame dancing under the dented pot. I really wanted her at the rink the first day. My guts were beginning to knot up already. What if the show failed and it was canceled after the first episode? Where would we be then? The poorhouse. Trent and his family and all his fabulous clothes would be in the pauper home, singing about picking a pocket or two.

"Okay, Mom, you can come sometime soon."

I *really* wanted our happy back.

FOUR

Dieter

_____

Car-sharing had seemed like a good idea at the time, only ending up with Stan and Arvy in the same car was excruciatingly loud this early in the morning.

Arvy was attempting to teach Stan some English, and the poor Russian seemed to think the louder he said a word the better. It didn't help that Arvy was driving and I was in the passenger seat, with Stan poking his head between the two of us so his shouting was right in my ear.

"I scored a goal," Arvy encouraged.

"I. Score. Goal!" Stan shouted, and raised his hands above his head in triumph. "Is good learn."

"It's a good thing to learn," Arvy corrected.

"Is good, I say," Stan said, and raised his hands again. "Score!"

By the time I arrived at the Rainbow Skate Arena, with its brightly painted welcome sign, my headache had grown exponentially, but I swallowed some meds and hoped it would be gone before I had to face Trent again.

Trent with his attitude, his smile, his dark eyes, and the makeup. I'd caught him staring at me a couple of times, but only because I'd been staring back. He was the absolute opposite of me; that was all I could think. He was a good six inches shorter, he was color and life where I was jeans and a Railers hoodie, he was a smile and I was a frown. I'd listened to what he hoped we'd learn from him, but I'd been compelled to ask him about what he'd learn from us. What could a bunch of loud, unfocused, post-season hockey players teach the tiny dancer?

"Think he'll teach us to pirouette?" Arvy asked, in all seriousness, as he laced up his skates.

"Pin ooh lette?" Stan said, latching onto the single word that was the hardest of all of them.

"Pi-roo-ett," Arvy corrected.

"Pi-roo-nayet." Stan repeated.

"Pirouette" was such a dainty word to be butchered so badly by our goalie that I had to laugh.

"Not laugh at me," Stan said with a frown, and poked me in the thigh. Which hurt, because shit, Stan was strong.

I held up both hands, protesting innocence. "I wasn't laughing at you, it's just that it's a really weird word," I began to explain, but saw Stan's bewildered look at my words. "Never mind."

Skates laced, I put on my under-armor, pulled the tapes nice and firm, then slipped on my jersey. Normally we'd be in practice jerseys for something like this, but the cameras wanted to see our names and numbers to build brand recognition. When I glanced around the room, at big Stan, at our very tall captain Hurleigh, at the slim but sturdy Ten, I could see we were all different, but maybe there was a theme here. Maybe we were all too similar for non-hockey fans to pick us apart.

I looked up as the door opened and Trent walked in, this time without his orange-clothed grandma at his side. There was no way anyone wouldn't know who he was. He was in what I guessed was his version of a practice jersey – form-fitting black pants and a dark gray shirt that was snug and had a hint of diamante on the V-neck. His hair was darker today, but his makeup was more flamboyant, his lip gloss scarlet, his eyes darkly lined. Cameras followed him in, and he was smiling at us.

Did anyone else in the room notice that the smile didn't quite reach his eyes? I tracked my gaze down his body, pausing momentarily at his groin. I pretended I was checking if he wore a cup, but mostly I knew exactly what I was doing. I carried on checking him out completely, from his strong thighs, to the muscles that showed in the pants, right down to his skates.

Not figure skates.

Hockey skates.

"You're wearing our gear," I blurted, because fuck if I have any control over my idiot mouth.

The cameraman moved and zoomed in on my face, and I tried my best to look neutral.

Trent glanced at me, then struck a pose in time for the camera to pan to him. "I need to feel what you do if I'm going to do this right," he answered, and ended with a nod and a seriously fine pout of his soft lips. He had this flamboyant thing down pat.

"Don't want you falling over," I said.

Why did I say that? Why didn't I just accept his answer and move on? Because it was all my fault what happened next.

He extended a hand. "Come with me."

I didn't really have a choice, because every eye was on me, and the cameraman had focused right back on my idiot face.

So I took his hand, and he led me out of the locker room and through a small corridor and out to the ice. This was obviously my first time on the ice at this rink, but it didn't matter – as soon as my blades were on the hard, cold stuff, I was at home. There were the markings of a hockey rink there, but no Plexiglas, just the oval.

And I was still holding his hand, which he was gripping hard. He pushed into a glide, and I followed his action, and soon we were skating smoothly in figure eights on the ice. He was wearing thin gloves, so I couldn't feel the warmth of his skin directly, but his hold was firm and sure, and he apparently wasn't scared of me falling on my heavy ass and taking him down with me.

"Don't even think of lifting me," I murmured when we were at the apex of the eight furthest from the camera.

He side-eyed me. "Likewise," he said, and there was a hint of a smile there, and this time it did reach his eyes. "Pick up some speed in the crossovers and then come to a fast stop in the middle."

"At center ice?" I asked for confirmation.

He nodded and let go of my hand, and I put on the speed that I knew I had, throwing in some accurate crossovers, then scraping the flat part of my blade on the ice and snowing to a dead stop right in the middle of the center ice circle.

I realized the camera had moved to Trent, who was repeating what I'd just done. Fancy footwork into the corner, and then he did this thing with his body – kind of a twist and a jump – and then he landed and snowed to a stop, his blades losing forward momentum literally an inch from mine. He'd just done the same as me, with added *dancing*, and he hadn't fallen on his ass without the toe picks he'd have on his usual skates.

"So I'm guessing you won't be falling over then," I deadpanned.

He put his hands on his slim hips and looked up at me. "Probably will," he said, "but I'll do it with style."

"No crashing into the boards, then," I said.

I didn't want the conversation to end, but by this time the rest of the team had joined me, and Trent slipped from being a cocky know-it-all with a teasing smile into professional mode. He waited until everyone was ranged around him, his only reaction when we all took a knee a slight raise of his eyebrow. I could tell he wanted to say something – likely an off-color comment about men on their knees – but he didn't. I thought about saying something to get a reaction, but it wasn't me who said inappropriate shit on this team – that was Adler Lockhart, with his ability to run his mouth without direction.

Anyway, my knee hurt.

"We're going back to basics," Trent announced. "I want film of all of you doing drills. Balance, glides, jumps, lunges, strides, crossovers, so I can do some prep work on where you need help."

I saw a couple of the players exchange pointed looks. I had this insane urge to poke them to listen to what he was saying, but I held myself back. One quelling look from the captain, and they stopped with the rolled eyes, but I felt the uneasy shit in Trent's audience. I guess none of us had expected we'd be faced with going back to peewee.

"Who wants to go first?"

Ten put up his hand, and dropped it immediately when his teammates, me included, shouted out things like "Suckup!" and "We're not in school!" I'd known it would be Ten who went first; the man was so damn eager to learn and improve all the time.

And he needs to improve. He's only here because of his name. He's not a fucking superstar.

I blinked away my thoughts and skated to the goal to

join the line. I wasn't at the front, I wasn't at the back; I was comfortably in the middle, right behind Stan. Being a goalie, Stan wasn't the greatest skater, but he could still move, and damn if we hadn't caught him doing a cart-wheel in the corridor before one of the playoff games. He was certainly agile.

Ten did all he was asked, pushing off, skating the figure eight, with deliberation at first, and then with raw speed. He glided, jumped, and did everything that was asked of him. He skated to a stop at the back of the queue like a kid who'd just done a water slide and was eager to go again. Freaking Boy Scout.

When it came to Stan's turn, he was a lot less graceful than Ten, but boy was he strong, an enormous presence on the ice. Only he didn't stop quite as well as he should have, and I saw the inevitable even as it was happening.

Contact between him and Trent, the smaller man flailing a little before Stan caught him and bodily lifted him off the ground like Scarlett in *Gone with the Wind*.

Stan looked hopelessly apologetic and Trent, small in his huge arms, looked a bit panicked before he replaced the shock with a fake laugh.

"We'll make a figure skater of you yet," Trent said for the cameras; a perfect soundbite.

Stan set him down, and he was grinning. "I help," he announced, and nodded like that was vitally important. Show-off.

I was up next, following exactly what everyone else had done, with my usual flair on the crossovers, confidence in the small jumps, building up speed and stopping dead one inch from Trent's skates. He didn't flinch, and I didn't apologize, and something passed between us. A flare of something – attraction, defiance, arousal? Fuck knew what it was, but this man was getting under my skin, and I couldn't take my eyes off his lips.

I should pick him up like Stan had. I could do that; he's light as air, and I probably bench-pressed his weight. And he'd look all kinds of pretty in my arms.

And in my bed, sprawled on the covers waiting for me to—

"Earth to Dieter… Move out the way, dude, it's my turn." Arvy was shoving at me, but I was staring, my fingers itching with the need to pick Trent up.

Then the shoving broke through the weirdness, and I joined the line at the back, waiting for my next turn.

Every so often, Trent looked over at me; sly, careful looks when he had his back to the camera. But I could see him, and I didn't look away.

He knew I wanted to pick him up. He had to know I wanted him in bed, his makeup smudged, his gloss smeared on my cock.

The session finished, and I wasn't winded or aching from too much work. I was just warmed up, and despite my aching knee I felt like we'd just done a leisurely family skate instead of a workout. The camera was in the room with us again, and part of me hoped that Trent was going to be sharing our space. No such luck – today was all about one-on-one talks to camera with the skaters about what they wanted from the training, and no sign of Trent at all.

I massaged my knee as I talked.

"I want to work on my speed," I announced. "I've seen other skaters work with guys like Trent, and I've seen how the way they hold themselves adds to their speed."

Not soon enough, they moved on to Stan, who tried to convey his enthusiasm and ended up relying on a thumbs-up. At least he couldn't butcher that one.

I excused myself and, back in my street clothes, I left

the locker room. I wasn't looking for Trent. I didn't want to see Trent. I had nothing to say to him. Or at least that was what I told myself.

I found him, though. In an office at the end of a long corridor, after following signs for the manager. I knocked on the open door, and he looked up in surprise. His makeup was still flawless, but he'd changed into this loose, flowing T-shirt that did nothing to hide the slim, toned man beneath.

He was wide-eyed for a second, then he relaxed back in his chair.

"Can I help?" he asked. "Is there something you need?"

You, I thought to myself, but didn't say that out loud.

"Do you do private lessons?" I asked, in a panicked moment of what-the-fuck-do-I-say.

He stood up from the desk, came around to the front, and sat on the edge of it.

"I have a contract. I'm not allowed to privately train anyone on the show."

Damn. That had been my way of getting some alone time with the sexy Trent. I moved closer to his desk, picking up a photo of him from the Sochi games.

"Silver," I summarized, and placed the picture back on the desk.

"You've never been called to play for…Germany, is it?"

"I can't imagine that happening," I said, with a huge dose of self-deprecation. I was dual nationality, German/Canadian, with a heavy bias on the Canadian. Still, it was Germany I would want to play for.

Come to think of it, the German national team would be my most likely option; Canada was kind of full.

"So," Trent started. I expected him to add something like "This is awkward", or something else that would fill the conversational emptiness. Then he went and shocked the hell out of me. "I was staring at you, and I want to feel like I can trust you enough that I could kiss you, but I don't. Sorry."

I blinked at him, lost for words. "What?"

He tilted his head and looked at me thoughtfully. "You're gay, right? Or bi? Or was I wrong?" He tensed a little, like he was expecting me to beat him up for the question.

"Bi," I answered, and I was staring back.

"I knew you were – I can tell when a man is assessing the size of my dick."

"Your ass," I corrected. "I was judging your ass."

Trent patted himself on the rear. "It's a good ass," he commented, like this was an everyday conversation.

"You have a high opinion of yourself," I said, not nastily, more to tease.

Sadness flittered across his face. "Someone has to have," he said.

We were at an impasse. I didn't know what to say, and he looked like he was a million miles away, lost in thoughts I had no access to.

Which was why, when he reached up and carded his fingers into my hair, went on tiptoes and kissed me gently on the lips, I went into a weird shock. I didn't move back in horror; equally I didn't deepen the kiss, and we parted with Trent looking up at me thoughtfully.

"So, we did that," he murmured.

"We did," was all I could think to say.

"It's done. It was okay. Nothing with sparks or anything."

He sounded like he was marking the kiss out of ten, or six, or however ice skating scoring worked. Full marks for confidence, only half for the kiss.

In a strong, determined move, I pulled him close and kissed him for real. Lips, tongues, and an inability to breathe. When we parted he was wide-eyed, his lip gloss smeared and his hands loose at his sides.

"That…" he began, but stopped.

I wiped away the stickiness of gloss from my lips and stepped back. Then my own kind of confidence came to the fore.

"Yeah," I said. "That was good."

And then I turned and left before someone walked in on us and saw me fucking Trent over the desk.

Because shit, that had been one hell of an explosive kiss.

FIVE

Trent

Four days later, and that kiss was still haunting me. It had been a stupid thing to do. I'd known that when I'd reached for Dieter and initiated things, yet it had felt so right at the time. Right but stupid. That could be the title of my autobiography. *Right but Stupid: The Trent Hanson Story* – available where books about misguided fucktards are sold."

The sigh that left me was legendary. I ended the tape of Tennant Rowe's skating talents. I'd been there in the manager's office of my rink for over an hour trying to concentrate and pick out where I thought the Railers needed work. Or perhaps I should say what I could add to their skating skills. I'd hidden myself away in this little stuffy cubicle to get some time away from the cameras. My gods, but I was tired of them already. It seemed as if I couldn't take a piss without someone with a camera or a makeup tote appearing at my side.

That morning had been a particularly bad one. I'd woken up as hard as a locust fence post and beaten off to a sultry fantasy that had involved my dick in Dieter Lehmann's ass. Knowing that the man was under my skin so deeply irked and titillated me. Maybe my irritation with myself for letting an ape like that into my fantasies was what had made the orgasm so intense. Yes. That was what we were going to say it had been.

Then the call from Mom at "really, mother" o'clock informing me that my stepfather, aka Voldemort, had called and begged her to go visit him and talk. The fact that she had to call me and see what I thought about the idea had lit me up like a Fourth of July firecracker. I hadn't yelled at her, of course, I'd merely tried my best to talk her out of going to see him. After the call had ended with her still fluctuating between saying no and saying yes, I'd ripped into my poor house like a dervish. I'd tossed my sewing room. *Tossed it.* Now I'd have to go home with a stupid camera crammed up my ass and set the area where I created my costumes to rights.

"Why are people such twats?" I asked the office. The AC hummed in reply.

I moved to the next video and groaned. Dieter was on my screen now. His power on those skates was undeniable, but he also could use some refinement. And my hands on his thighs...parting them so I could wiggle between them and take what I was sure was a fat, long cock into my mouth and suck him so hard and so well he passed out from the pleasure.

Voices slipped into the porn reel in my mind. I jerked my hand from my crotch, aghast at being so weak-willed, and cocked my head slightly. Was someone singing "Fox on the Run" while someone else hissed at them to stop? No one was supposed to be there for another thirty minutes.

I pushed myself from the hard chair I'd been moping

and daydreaming in and peeked around the door of my rink manager's office. There in the corridor, alone, were Layton Foxx and Adler Lockhart.

Adler was the singer, if that was what you wanted to call the caterwauling. Layton was waving a hand at the hockey player as if trying to quiet the man. Then Lockhart leaned into Foxx, pressing him gently against the wall and kissing him as if he hadn't eaten in days.

Well, now. Looked like Tennant, Jared and Dieter weren't the *only* ones on the team who were marching under the rainbow flag.

I leaned on the doorframe and watched the passionate moment. When they broke apart, Foxx caressed Lockhart's face so lovingly it made me ache. Being a sour little queen, I cleared my throat. Adler leaped back as if he'd just painfully discovered a hornet in his cup. Foxx spun to look at me. I wiggled a couple of fingers at the lovers.

"You may wish to have your assignations in a more private place. May I suggest this office?" I waved a gloved hand at the room behind me.

"Look, it wasn't what you think it was," Adler stammered.

I cocked a slim eyebrow.

"Okay, it was what you thought it was, but please don't out us."

"Oh my gods. Do I look like the type of man who would out other men? Please." I walked down to where they stood like a pair of petrified trees. "Just be careful if you're hiding this relationship. I mean it about the cameras. They followed me home and taped me sitting on the couch watching TV. They even asked if they could film me talking to my mother about the scandal. Maybe she's smart to keep her distance from this whole fiasco."

"Christ," Foxx murmured.

I nodded.

"Thank you for being so..."

"Gay and understanding? My pleasure. Now go off and be happy lovers somewhere else. The kids will be arriving shortly, and so will the damn cameras."

Adler slapped my shoulder so hard I winced. "You're a good guy even if you do wear lipstick the same color as my mom."

Layton groaned and took his affable kissing-mate off by the hand, the social media man's mouth going a mile a minute.

How wonderful it would be to have someone to scold about silly little social gaffes. I slipped back into that tiny office, closed the door, and spent the next forty minutes watching Dieter on ice. By the time the children were ready for me, I was a hot mess, but I put on my makeup and my performing smile and I sashayed out onto the ice like the fucking star I was. My skaters – the kids ranging in ages from six to sixteen – all applauded and gathered around me.

"Look at you all," I gushed, hugging as many as I could. Some, like Scotty the ten-year-old transgender girl, were exceptionally special to me, but I adored them all. "Are you going to give the TV show cameras your best today?" I asked, moving through the adoring fans to get a last-minute costume and make-up check. They all shouted yes. They made me so proud.

It had been decided that I'd do one of my short programs from Sochi and then work with the kids, bringing in the Railers to show how harmonious we all were and how inclusive ice sports now were. Which was a huge pile of steaming shit. I remembered all too well the scathing remarks made about me by TV announcers – who were

retired figure skaters – during my silver-medal performance. I'd been called many terrible things since I'd first
come out about liking boys at a tender age, but what those
announcers had said about me being too feminine and too
odd to be associating with young boys still turned my stomach. It had made me cry back then, and it would today
given my state of mind if I'd only let it. But I refused to
give shitful people like that the pleasure of seeing my tears.
Besides, my skaters needed Trent to be Trent. And so, for
them, I was always brave in public and shed the tears in
private.

"We need to get this jacket up just a bit more," I told
Gayle. She pulled out box of pins from her purse – she was
learning how to agent a figure skater well – and began
pinning the hem of the short white jacket. "If it's too low it
hides the curvature of my ass."

"Hold still before I jab you." She worked quickly.

I smiled at the children, then found the hockey players
lined up on the other side of the boards. I could feel Dieter
before I could see him. I knew his eyes were on my ass,
which was why I had to make sure that it was viewable.

"Are you feeling better?" Gayle asked.

"Yes," I lied. "Thank you for coming over and talking
to me this morning. You're an angelic agent," I whispered
as some tall man with a bun and garlic breath touched up
my eyeliner and gloss. As if it needed touching up. I knew
how to apply, thank you.

"Remember that when the producers of the show ask
to go on a date with you." She smiled at me, then gave the
sparkly white jacket a firm tug. "There. All pinned and
high enough to show off that pert ass. Now go show the
people at home why you won that silver medal."

We bussed cheeks, then I skated out to center ice,
inhaled, artfully raised my arms over my head, dug my toe

pick into the ice and waited for the music. It was one of my favorite routines, performed to "Carmen", and showcased my flair and strengths. As soon as the music began, my mind went to the routine – the jumps, the sass that signaled that Trent Hanson was performing this skate. Through the salchows and lutzes, the toe loops and axels, I felt hot, steady eyes on me. Knowing Dieter was right there, engrossed by my ability and my body, feeling his hungry eyes on me as I worked my magic, made me feel light-headed and giddy. Combined with the sheer joy of ice and music, when I ended with an impromptu Johnny Weir slide, the darkness of the morning had lifted.

The kids boiled out onto the ice like ants from a hill. They were followed by the Railers. My gaze locked with Dieter's, and the rest of the hoopla melted away like spring snow. He wanted me. Right now. I could see it in his eyes. I wanted him just as badly. That kiss and all the sexual promise it held mixed with the churning emotions inside me left me in a state of heightened bubbliness.

The next hour was remarkable and torturous. I loved my kids and my rink, and I was beginning to like the apes on skates as well. The Railers were wonderful with the kids, laughing and showing them that they also had skate prowess. Adler and a few others picked up the smaller figure skaters and raced around the rink with them. There was so much laughter and happiness that I knew I'd be frothing over like a freshly popped bottle of champagne when we left the ice.

And I was. See how well I know myself.

"Let's all gather together and go somewhere to eat. The studio will pay for it!" I announced in my most spirited voice. The show producers began to balk, but the chance of us all being out and getting the public's reaction was just too much for them to pass up. "I'll just slip into the locker room and change. Can someone run to Dan's office – he's the rink manager – and get my street clothes from the chair in the corner?"

And just like that I found myself waiting in the men's locker room for Dieter Lehmann to come back with my city togs. I removed the white skates and placed them neatly by my feet, folded my hands in my lap, and waited. He appeared not two minutes later, filling the doorway and then the damn locker room with his broad shoulders and appealing sulking demeanor.

"Bring them to me," I said flatly, my hands still lying in my lap.

He seemed to be locked into some kind of internal battle. Maybe he wasn't used to a man who was so much smaller than him being so pushy and domineering. If he knew me better, he'd know that I'm *always* pushy and domineering. As well as a few other less than flattering terms.

Finally, his big feet broke free and he walked my clothes to me. I remained seated, but my eyes traveled up his body. He looked edible in that blue jersey and jeans. His eyes were smoldering green and gold embers that never moved from my face.

Funny how what I reached for wasn't my trousers, dress shirt and sleek blue vest. Maybe my reaching for his belt and pulling him to me wasn't funny at all. Maybe it was chapter two in my stupid book. Probably. But oh, how my body hummed with desire the closer he came. I brushed my nose against his jersey and drew in deeply. He smelled like dark sandalwood and mystery with a dash of sex. Just my type. Add in a sprinkling of heartbreak and you'd have all my past lovers. But who cares? One quick blowjob in the locker room wouldn't hurt anything. So I slid off the bench, so hot to have him come down my throat that the knowledge that I was ruining the white knees of my skating slacks had no impact. That was how bad I had it.

"What are you doing?" he asked, his voice thick and smoky.

I tugged down his fly and slid my hand inside his briefs. The backs of my fingers brushed a wet spot on the cool cotton of his underwear. Someone had been aroused for a long time. That knowledge made my dick throb in time with my rapid pulse. Out came his cock. I had been right. It was fat and long. Hard, too, and slick with precum.

"Do you really not know?" I asked before I licked the round head of his cock clean. He sucked in a sharp breath, my clothes still in his hands.

He groaned. "Hurry up. I've been hard for fucking hours because of you."

"Only hours?" I rolled my tongue around him, pressing on the knot of nerves under the head of his cock. My fingers held the base of his dick firmly. I felt the shudder that rolled through all those powerful muscles.

"Days. Ever since that kiss. Shit, Trent, stop teasing and suck me off before someone walks in." He thrust his hips outward, his cock sliding from my lips across my cheek. "I dreamed of seeing that gloss of yours smeared on my cock."

I turned my head to swallow him down, eager and hungry, I took him as deeply as I could.

"Fuuuuuuck."

There was no time for finesse. We both knew that. He tossed my clothes aside and slid his hands into my hair.

"Gelled, too. You're high maintenance, aren't you? I bet you are. I think I could get into that."

I had too much cock in my mouth to reply. He didn't really seem to be searching for an answer. He just started pumping, and I started sucking as hard as I could, my hands on his hips urging him to fuck my mouth.

His final thrust made my eyes water. I swallowed greedily, pulling off the best I could to ensure all that cum didn't go down my throat. I wanted some on my tongue. I needed to savor the taste of the man. He released his hold on my head and watched as I pulled off his prick then licked him clean, my hand still wrapped around him.

I got him as clean as I could, then sat back on my calves, glanced upward, and used the tip of my index finger to dab at the corners of my mouth.

Dieter just stared down at me, his chest still heaving and his eyes glassy from lust. I still wanted the man. The head I've just given him had been an appetizer.

"Are you shocked?" I asked, then shoved his still-wet cock back into his jeans and carefully zipped him back up.

"I've never been with a man like you." He offered me his hand.

I took it and he tugged, getting me up off my knees quickly. "There *are* no other men like me."

He smiled. It was akin to someone pulling back the drapes on what had been a room filled with mourners and allowing life to reenter. It rocked me to the core and set off about four hundred warning bells. A man this stunning with so many dark corners was bad news. Bad, bad, bad news.

"Yeah, I believe that," he replied, and swept in to take a kiss that ended with me flat against the wall and his hands down the front of my white spandex pants. "I want to get at you now. You good for that?"

"God, yes," I panted, then nipped at his bottom lip. We'd have been rutting like wild beasts had his cell not rung at that moment. "Ignore it. I need your mouth on me." I grabbed fistfuls of hair and pulled his mouth back to mine. The damn phone kept ringing. He leaned into me, pressing all that firm hockey player against my chest. I was finding it hard to breathe. I was fucking loving it.

"Yo, Deet, man, you coming or what?"

The sound of his name rolling out of one of his team-mates doused the fire well. Dieter danced away from me, his face flushed and his pupils so large it was hard to see any color at all. I spun around to try to do something with the stiff dick tenting my pants, but there was nothing to be done with it. The dance belt I wore under my skating pants didn't hide erections well. Maybe I needed one with more padding…

"Yeah, I'm just waiting for Trent," he shouted, then jogged to the door to block off whoever it was who had come looking for him. "He's taking a shower."

"Oh, okay." I ran in the direction of the showers and hid behind a cool tiled wall. "We'll meet you at the restaurant. It's a Brazilian steakhouse over on Chestnut Street that Trent's agent said is the hot new spot to be seen at, so the show is all behind us getting there now."

"Right, okay. We'll find it on Google maps. Catch you later, Arvy."

"You okay? You sound spacey."

"I'm good."

The conversation faded off. I let my eyes close and rested my brow on the tiles. Then I heard him come around the corner. I lifted my head and opened my eyes. He pushed the pile of my clothes at me.

"I still want to get at you," he informed me.

I took the clothes from him and wet my lips. His gaze settled on my mouth. "I still want you to get at me."

With that, I slipped around him, wrinkled outfit in hand, and left him staring at my ass. The ball – or I guess that would be a puck – was in his court. At his end of the ice. Whatever. I suck at making sporty witticisms but excel at leaving men wanting more. I chanced an over-the-shoulder peek, just to be sure, and saw that his sight was riveted to my ass. Mm-hmm. As I thought. His gaze darted up to ensnare mine. This was going to turn into *way* more than just a quick BJ in the locker room; I could feel it riding the air currents like a line of summer storms.

SIX

Dieter

W hat I really wanted *right the hell then* was to follow Trent into the shower, but that would have been taking too much of a risk. What if one of my teammates walked in on us?

Not that I cared what people thought of who I chose to have sex with, but the whole 'having sex in the team showers' thing wasn't exactly fair.

So I sat and waited, and twenty minutes after he went in, Trent appeared at the door to the showers, fully dressed – much to my disappointment – and brushing damp hair from his face. He'd rimmed his eyes in that black again, but there was no lip gloss. That disappointed me on a visceral level. His gloss had tasted of strawberry and slicked our kissing, and the fact that it was smeared on my cock was an image and sensation I would carry to my grave as a highlight.

Jeez, the man was a temptation in tight pants.

"Come here," he said, and crossed to the mirrors with the hair driers. Like a puppy, I did as I was told – anything to get up close and personal. He switched on the nearest hairdryer, aiming it at his hair, his hands moving in some kind of rhythm that had him styling at the same time as rough-drying. "Kiss me," he mouthed over the noise of the drier.

I didn't say no. Cradling his face, I kissed him as he dried his hair, and it didn't matter what he was doing – he could clearly multitask, because the kissing was hot.

And then we parted and he turned to the mirror. A few flicks of his fingers, and his hair was perfect. He pouted at his reflection, slicked gloss onto his lips, ran the tip of his index finger along the black to smudge around his eyes, then he turned to me.

"Think I'm ready for my closeup?"

I was lost for words. How had I lived twenty-five years without having something as perfect as Trent? How had I been into men for at least ten of those years and never wanted to kiss a man like him, with his colorful flamboyance and take-charge persona? I was hard, so damn hard, and I palmed my cock in a very deliberate motion. All Trent did was smirk, the fucker.

I followed him out of the changing area; a quick glance at Trent in tight jeans had me reaching for him without thinking. Then I stopped. There were cameras here, and we needed to do the promo thing.

We found the restaurant, no more than a ten-minute walk from the rink, and the entire way I walked to the right and just slightly behind Trent. I was his bodyguard, and I saw the second looks he got. They could be because he was famous, or because he wore a flowing scarlet shirt you could see right through to the tight-T-shirt beneath. Who knew? He didn't appear to notice any of them, but I can guarantee you that they all saw me behind him, glowering at each and every one of them.

He opened the door for me, which was something I

wasn't used to, but I didn't argue, simply stepped in and headed directly for the table where the rest of the Railers sat. There was a space next to Arvy, and I took it, aware that the only other spare seat was down near Stan. That put an entire table length between us, which was probably the safest thing to do. Cameras moved around the table, and I got a sense of what they were looking for. Mostly Trent, who laughed brightly up at huge, muscled Stan who took up nearly two chairs. Trent was tiny next to him, and I could tell from some of the angles the camera guys used that they were focusing on that difference.

"I hope Stan doesn't fall off his chair and squash the kid," Arvy said from my side, leaning back in his chair and patting his belly. He'd somehow managed to down the largest steak served in the place, whereas I was only halfway through my dinner.

I knew why. I was all riled up, and blown away, and needy, and clearly that played havoc with a man's appetite.

"He's not a kid," I said, and forked in another piece of steak. It was melt-in-your-mouth delicious, like I didn't need to chew, even though I actually did so I looked normal.

Arvy leaned into me. "Looks like a kid at the grown-up table," he said under his breath.

I side-eyed him and hoped to hell the cameras hadn't caught that comment or my reaction. "He's sitting at a table of giants," I said back.

Arvy grimaced and rubbed his belly again. "I need to hit the gym early in the a.m. –, you with me?"

I wanted a lot of things at that moment, but working in the gym at some ungodly hour wasn't on the list.

"Earth to Deets, come in Deets."

"What?" I asked, focusing back on Arvy and away

from Trent, who was doing something impossibly cute and incredibly sexy with his steak knife.

"I said gym, six, I'll bang on your door?"

We were all at the Philadelphia Club Hotel on Chestnut Street, a fairly standard room setup, but a hotel with an extensive gym and a pool.

"Yeah," I said, and concentrated back on my steak.

I half hoped Trent would give me some kind of subtle sign that suggested we'd go back to his place, wherever that was, and fuck like rabbits, but if he did, then I missed it. When he left at just after ten, after stealing a mouthful of Stan's dessert and making everyone laugh when Stan got all grumpy and Trent had to tease him out of it, I was bereft.

No, not bereft – disappointed, maybe. All I had to do was recall Trent's mouth on me and I was a goner. I really wanted more.

THE NEXT DAY wasn't any better. The gym was brutal, because it seemed like every part of me ached. I took two pills for the knee ache, but I stopped after that. I wanted to be sharp for Trent, to lure him somewhere quiet and listen to his voice as he told me what he wanted. Unfortunately, I didn't get to talk to him privately.

That morning's session was all about angles and balance, and Trent, in sapphire blue from head to toe, picked on Stan as an example.

He spoke into the cameras as he fussed around the big Russian.

"Stan is the goalie and has impressive stretch and reach, he can move on a dime, but his skating is hampered by the gear he has to wear."

"So what can you do for him?" the interviewer asked Trent, looking from Stan back to Trent as he talked.

"He's mentioned that he wants more explosive power in his legs, the kind of thing we have as figure skaters when we're jumping into spins, and I just want to work with that this morning."

He had us all jumping literally like ballerinas, which some of the guys, including me, found hilarious. A couple were too embarrassed to try, which the interviewer loved. There was some in-depth questioning about why they were embarrassed – I think they were hoping for one of the guys to say they weren't going to do some girlie jumps. Arvy just explained he was scared of falling on his ass in front of the camera. Stan looked pointedly at his gear and raised a single eyebrow to explain why he didn't want to jump as high as Trent wanted him to.

Of course, by the end of the session both men were channeling Baryshnikov and jumping like pros. Every one of my muscles ached, and fishing out painkillers was mere muscle memory because my knee hurt. I had to schedule in some PT, and I should talk to the team about someone here, a local. I took double because two didn't work for me anymore, and I tried not to think that I was lying to myself, but let's be honest, my very clever and tricky brain had decided I needed as much as I could take and I had to get on taking them right now.

The sense of wellbeing was there nice and quick, and my knee muscles relaxed. Next session I would strap the damn thing up. If I'd done that, I wouldn't be in pain right now.

"You're up for the one-on-one interview," Adler said, looking at his clipboard. He did that a lot – crossing and ticking and generally taking control of his skaters, as he liked to call us.

"Me? Really? Isn't it Arvy's turn?" I wasn't in the mood, and Trent had caught my eye earlier and winked. I really wanted a piece of whatever he was teasing me about.

I must have sounded like I knew what I was talking about, because Adler looked back at his list with a frown. I felt the anticipation of leaving early and seeking out Trent. Then Adler looked at me over his clipboard.

"Nope. You're up. Arvy is tomorrow, and no, I'm not swapping you out. Go talk nice."

I cursed under my breath and saw Trent's lips twitch. Asshole.

The interview was standard stuff. What was I hoping to learn, what had I learned already, and how was the training impacting me as a hockey player? I answered everything clearly, as much as I could, anyway, when my head began to feel like it was stuffed with cotton wool halfway through. I must have done okay, because they wrapped it all up quickly, and when I went back into the changing room to collect my bag, most people had gone.

"Beer back at the hotel," Arvy announced as he left.

I nodded, the wooliness becoming something else – a dizzy sickness that had me sitting down in the stall I'd been assigned. I leaned back against the wall after everyone had gone, looking up at ceiling and willing the room to stop spinning. My head felt too big for my body, and a sensation as if fire ants crawled under my skin. I scratched at each point, my hands slipping in something wet. I looked down at where I'd been brushing at the ants I couldn't see, and I saw scarlet. Blood on my skin. Where had that come from?

I closed my eyes, my fingers pressing at every itchy part.

"What the hell?"

I tried to open my eyes, but my brain was telling me not to look at Trent, who was likely standing there looking at me as if I was a moron. Who the hell scratched through their skin? Who would sit there with ants under their skin and their head spinning like a Catherine wheel?

"Dieter?" Trent said, and he'd moved. He was crouching between my legs. "What did you take? Talk to me, Dieter. Do I need to call 911?"

That had me opening my eyes, and after a few seconds I could focus on Trent's face. His hair was wet, he didn't have makeup on, and he looked so young. I wanted to touch him, but my hands wouldn't move.

"No 911, I'm okay," I enunciated carefully. Speaking normally when under the influence was a particular skill of mine, or so I liked to think.

"Dieter, what is it? What did you take?"

I shook my head, or my head shook me, or…I didn't know what the hell was going on. This wasn't right. The meds made me happy, relaxed my sore muscles – they didn't make me feel like I was being turned inside out.

"Is it these?" Trent said, and waved something in front of my face. "How many? Two? Four? More?"

"Six," I managed. That was right – two before, then two more, then another two…or was it more? No, it was six, so why was I feeling like this?"

"Okay," I heard Trent say on a loud exhale. "We ride this one out."

He sat next to me. I knew he was there, I felt his hand on my leg, and I wanted to hold his hand, but instinct told me I shouldn't do that.

I don't know how long it took, or how long we sat there. I heard voices, Trent explaining I was ill and we were waiting for a cab, another voice saying something about lights. I wasn't following it all, just focusing on Trent.

Finally, the dizziness stopped, the fiery itching ceased, and I could focus on the cold towel he'd obviously placed over the worst of the scratches, and the fact that I was sitting next to Trent. He'd removed his hand from my leg and was checking his phone.

I could see what he was looking at, and it filled me with dread. Headlines about addiction, painkillers, hockey. I could see them as he scrolled through the Google search.

"Hey," I said, softly, because I didn't really want him to speak to me.

He looked at me, clearly startled, his brown eyes wide. He'd evidently not left my side, his once wet hair dry and in soft layers around his face. His expression was a strange mix of concerned and pissed.

"Tell me you didn't know what dosage you were taking?" he said, without explanation.

Great, diving right on into my fucked up habit.

"They're for my knee," I said.

"*Your* knee?" he asked, like he doubted me.

"Yeah."

"So your name isn't Dieter, then, it's actually Alain Poulin." He shook the bottle in front of me. "Because if your name is Dieter, then these aren't your pills."

I was trapped. How did I explain that one away? Alain had been a teammate down in the AHL, and the Percocet had been left over from an operation on a herniated disc. I'd paid for them; post-op meds were easy to come by if you had the money or the connections.

I snatched the pills from Trent, which took two goes as my coordination was still for shit.

"They're mine," I stated, and poked them back into my bag, the damp cloth slipping from my arm and exposing the red raw scratches.

"Like ants crawling under your skin," Trent said. "I know that because pumping yourself full of meds isn't just a hockey thing, you know."

A kernel of hope sat in my chest. Was it possible that I wouldn't need to defend myself, that maybe Trent had experienced what I had? He blew that idea out of the water with his next words.

"I had a partner who wrecked his knee trying for a triple. He finally managed to kick the addiction."

He looked at me accusingly, like I was a lesser person who relied on these fucking tablets.

"I'm not addicted," I defended myself immediately. "I have pain and I must have taken too many."

"Eight. You told me eight, and this is the strong stuff."

"Six," I amended. I was sure I'd only got to six.

Trent stood up, brushing his pants. "Okay, take care," he said, his voice sounding a little off.

"What?" I stood up as well, using the wall to hold me.

"I'll see you tomorrow," he added, and left.

"Trent!" I called out as he reached the door.

"What?" he asked, but didn't turn around.

"We should talk."

At that point, he did turn and face me, but gone was the serious expression, and in its place was the mask he used for the press. That benign smile that hid so much.

"Another time, darling," he drawled, and walked out.

"Then fuck you," I called after him, before sitting down abruptly. What the hell had I called that out for?

I pulled the plastic bottle of pills out of the bag, looked at the label for the first time. I'd just assumed they were the standard shit, but these were extra strength – no wonder I'd felt like hell.

Well, I'd felt like shit *after* that amazing feeling of being able to conquer anything.

I gripped the bottle hard and walked into the shower area and over to the sinks. For the longest time, I held the bottle over the sink, imagining the pills vanishing down the plughole. Then I remembered how nice it had felt to take them, before Trent's expression forced its way right there into the front of my thoughts. Why did Trent's opinion matter I didn't know, but I knew one thing.

I'm not an addict.

"I'm fucking disgusting," I snapped, and tipped every last one of them into the sink, forcing them down the plughole, crushing them with my room keycard, probably wrecking the damn thing in the process.

What fucking right did Trent have to look at me like that?

I'm not an addict.

Not anymore.

SEVEN

Trent

_____

My gods, it was Jonah all over again.

I flew past the cameraman lounging by the locker rooms. I knew he was supposed to follow me around that afternoon. I was scheduled to visit my favorite spa, which I really couldn't afford but, show business... and get my usual tidy up below the belt as well as a facial and a mani-pedi. That was not happening now. No way in hell could I flounce around spreading my rays of sunshine in this mood. I was frantic and manic and on the verge of a breakdown of biblical proportions.

"Hey, wait up," Chet said. Was his name Chet? Rhett? Gomez? Who the fuck cared? I was growing to despise the cameras and the people associated with them. "I'm supposed to go with you. Ginger said we were doing the spa and then you were supposed to go to this gay fundraiser over at the Rittenhouse Manor Hotel."

I spun around and held up one finger. Just one. Damn, I really did need a manicure. "Do not follow me. I mean it, Gomez."

"Chet," mumbled the portly man in the Flyers cap.

"What. Ever. Do not follow me. I'm not in a good place."

"But the show…"

"Fuck the show."

With that, I twirled around and stormed out of my rink, the soft blue scarf I'd tied artfully around my throat wafting out behind me. My exit would have made Cher proud had my fucking scarf not gotten caught in the fucking door. The tug when I reached the end nearly garroted me. Chet stood on the other side of the glass doors, staring, camera in hand, wearing his orange ball cap as the door and I battled over my scarf.

"You're a miserable sow-faced bitch!" I screamed at the door as I pulled and tugged.

Chet tentatively reached out and pushed the door open. I whipped my scarf free, twirled on my saucy booted heel, and stalked off, tears forming and blurring my departure. I could make out the shape of my yellow Yamaha scooter through the haze of unshed tears.

"Dammit to hell," I coughed, then unlocked my helmet and shoved it down onto my head.

I probably shouldn't be driving at all in this mental state, but I had to get away from Dieter and the pills and the whole addiction thing. I just could not do that again. Swiping at tears as I rode through city traffic, I purposefully blocked out all memories of Jonah, his struggles with prescription pills, and the agony of being part of that cycle.

"I barely know the man," I told myself as I scooted to Liberty Nails & Manicures, the shop where my mother worked.

She and *Lola* knew all about Jonah. They'd gone through that with me. They'd seen the agony, gone through the t911 calls numerous times. They'd lived with the calls and the pleading, the fights, the weeping, the promises of going straight and the broken vows that had always followed.

I was so desperate to see her and talk to her that I didn't even take off my yellow helmet to fluff up my hair. Gina, the owner, looked up from a customer's soaking fingers when I blew into the busy shop. I gave the place a quick once-over and didn't see my mother.

"Hello, Trent," she called. All the women in the shop greeted me. "If you're looking for your mother, she didn't come in today."

I hurried over to the petite blonde and dropped into a crouch. Her customer smiled warmly.

"What do you mean, she didn't come in?"

"She went up to Mercer to see Clay."

I simply crouched there, blinking, like an idiot.

"Thanks, Gina."

I eventually pushed out, stood up, and exited the shop filled with curious women. My head was a complete wreck. I sat on my scooter parked by the curb and stared at the street. Shimmering heat waves were already rising from the blacktop. She'd gone to see him. Taken a day off to see the man who'd fucked us all over. Why? Why would she do that? Why would she skip work to see Clay – that fucktard – but not take a day to be on my show? Why? It made no sense. We hated Clay. My stepfather was a shitty man who had ruined us. Why was she there visiting him?

I started my scooter and went home. Not to my place. To *Lola*. As soon as my grandmother saw me, hair flat, eyeliner smudged across my cheeks, and hiccupping as I tried not to cry, she pulled me into a huge hug. And there we stood, in that tiny kitchen with the smells of soy, garlic and curry in the air. Me weeping like a tiny wee baby boy and her whispering soothing words in Pilipino.

"Come sit down, babes," *Lola* murmured, leading me to a chair that creaked when I dropped into it. She pit-pattered around as I cried into my hands. "Here, here. Stop crying. What has you so bad upset?"

She lifted my face upward, then pressed a wet, cold dishcloth to my cheek.

"Everything. Just – everything."

I grabbed the towel and shoved my face into it. The coolness felt good on my cheeks. It helped me calm down a bit. She was seated across from me when I emerged from the wet dishtowel. In front of me was a huge mug of ginger tea.

"*Lola*, I'm not sick. I don't need *salabat* tea," I coughed as I peeked at her.

"You sick at heart. Drink tea." She folded her arms over her Flyers T-shirt. Different day, different Flyers shirt. This one had a 16 on it and the name CLARKE across the back. She'd had one like it since the mid-seventies.

The ginger tea was so strong I gagged, but the taste made me feel somewhat better even if it was killing me slowly. It brought back simpler days when I was a kid and had a cold. Anytime you sneezed, you got a mug of *salabat* tea.

"I feel like my whole life is upside-down," I sniffled into my tea. The mug was warm and soothing between my palms.

"What makes it upside-down? Man trouble?"

Lola pushed a plate of store-bought cookies toward me. I shook my head but took one anyway. What difference did it make if I gained weight? Not like I'd ever be skating again. That last show in Harrisburg had been the finale of my contracted appearances. Guessed that dream of doing an eighties ice extravaganza show would die now along with all my other hopes and dreams.

"I barely know the man. I mean, we shared one blow — intimate moment, and a few kisses. Why should I go there again?"

"Go where?"

"Into the hell that is a drug-addict boyfriend."

I dunked my cookie in my tea, then shoved it whole into my face. The sugar tasted amazing. So I grabbed another cookie and did the same. It melted on my tongue. Hot, yes, but so incredible and forbidden for *so* many years that I didn't care if I scalded all my taste buds.

"You have a new boyfriend?" She pouted.

I hurried to explain – or try to explain – before her heart broke in two. "No, we're not that. At all. We're attracted and we kissed once or twice."

"And made blowjobs."

"*Lola!*"

"What? You think I don't know two gay boys suck dick?"

I grabbed two more cookies and ate them as my grand-mother patiently waited.

"No, I know you know what gay boys do. It's just…" I sighed and told her the story of Dieter and me, sparing no detail aside from sexual ones. "And then I left. No, please, don't give me bad looks."

"You leave man who needs help? You okay to suck his dick but not be his friend when he needs you?" Her silver eyebrows were tangled. I lowered my head, then ate another cookie. "Trenton, we raise you better."

"I know, but I can't do that again. I can't suffer with another addict. Jonah nearly killed me."

"Jonah nearly kill himself. Four times I know."

I peeked up through my flat bangs. She was showing me four fingers.

"So you run off from Dieter because he makes you scared? When does being scared make you run?"

"Since my world is in tatters. I don't think I can fight anymore, *Lola*." I ate another cookie.

"Shit balls. You fight since you were eight and Clay tell you only sissy boys sew skating clothes." She leaned over the table, her substantial breasts resting on her age-spotted forearms. I met her gaze. "You remember what you tell asshole Clay when he tell you boys no sew?"

I did recall that moment. I just didn't want to admit that I did. I shook my head.

"You tell Clay that boys can sew if they want. You stood up to him and you been fighting bigot people ever since. You want to tell skater kids to no fight?"

"*Lola*, that's different," I whined. And ate another cookie.

She leaned back in her chair, her mouth pulled into a tight pucker. Damn. She was upset with me now. I knew that face.

"I never think I see the day that my famous gay grandson would stop fighting. All the kids will be sad." She shook her head, and shame swept over me.

"It scares me," I whispered. "I look at this man and I think I could care about him. People who care do stupid things. Look at Mom!" I waved a finger at her. "She went to see Clay; did you know that?"

"I know. I tell her not to, but she loves him."

"How? How can she love a man who did that to her? How can she go see the man who robbed us and left us teetering on the verge of financial ruin? It makes no sense!" I ate two more cookies, chewing angrily.

Lola shrugged. "People in love do stupid things." She took a sip of her ginger tea and sighed as if in bliss. Her eyes met mine over my mug. "Do you love this man?"

"No, no, it's nothing near that yet." I reached for a cookie and was shocked to find the plate empty. Well, hell. Right to my ass was where all of *those* would go. "It could be something, though. I'm incredibly attracted to him. We're just sort of friends. Yes, friends. We're just friends. Mostly. He has lovely eyes, *Lola*. Green with bursts of amber around the pupils. Such a stunning man." I could see Dieter in my mind's eye, a smile playing on his usually brooding face. A shiver of something primal and powerful traveled over me. There could be something there. Oh yes. "But then there's the pills…"

"Maybe he needs help from a friend who gives blowjobs."

"Maybe," I conceded as my cheeks reddened a bit. "What about Mom? What are we going to do about her?"

"We're going to let her make her own mistakes, babes. Same as we do for you. Want more cookies?"

"Will you sit and talk with me while I eat them?"

She smiled so widely her wrinkled cheeks nearly hid her deep brown eyes. "You know *Lola* always here for my babes."

"Yeah, I know." I reached over the empty cookie plate and threaded my fingers into hers. "I know."

I TRACKED him down at his hotel. It was easy. I just called Adler Lockhart, the man I'd seen kissing Layton Foxx. He was happy to tell me what room Dieter was in, as well as some story about a goat followed by a joke about a lima bean going to confession. This would be stop one on the Tough Talk Tours. After I was done setting Dieter straight, it was back home to lie in wait for my mother and confront her as well. Yep. Watch Trent fight back.

A couple of hours ago, fueled up by *Lola*'s tea, cookies, and motivational talk, this had seemed like a *grand* idea. Go see Dieter with food in hand – that was *Lola*'s idea – and tell him that I would help him as much as I could but that I could *not* get more involved with him. Friends. We would just be friends. Maybe with a few benefits. Sucking his dick had been incredible. I'd bet he'd be lively as a bottom or a top. I was happy with either.

Imagine that long, fat cock being slowly pushed into—

"Trent, for the love of all the gods, stop it," I hissed at myself, and knocked sharply on the door of room 22-B.

Friends. Just friends. No dick sucking. No kissing. Absolutely no cocks in anyone's ass. Nope. No. None of that. Friends. A man helping a man who was struggling. Me being a good soul. Someone fetch me a *freaking* merit badge.

The door opened. I looked up and saw Dieter's expression shift from morose to ecstatic in the span of a heartbeat. There was that smile again. The one that showed off a small dimple on his right cheek. The one that cut through the dark fog of fear and unease like a beacon from a lighthouse. The smile that made me stammer and look stupid.

"Food." I lifted the insulated tote that *Lola* had filled with home-cooked goodness, and offered it to him. "I mean my grandmother made us food. For a picnic. Inside. Where no one can see us talking. We need to talk."

"Oh, wow, this is great." He flung the door wide open.

I sucked in a deep breath, smelled Dieter and dark sandalwood, and knew my boat was headed for rocky shores, to keep with the whole lighthouse/maritime motif my mind was stuck in.

"I'm really glad to see you."

I turned, purple tote from the local market in hand, as

the door closed. "I was rude to you and I need to apologize."

Dieter shook his head. "No, you don't need to do that. I shouldn't have laid all that on you."

"No," I argued. "I need to sit down and explain why I acted like I did. I also want to offer you my friendship to help you get through your problems with pills."

"It's all good." He smiled widely.

My aft hit the rocks. Aft. Was that the front of a boat? Who knew? Sailors, I'd wager. Pity I'd never piloted a ship before. Which explained why mine was already taking on water.

"I dumped them all down the drain. I'm done with them. I'm clean."

I heard what he was saying, I just couldn't make myself believe I was hearing it. I looked around, found the dresser, and placed the tote carefully on top of it. Then I unwrapped my scarf – the one I'd torn slightly in the tussle with the doors of my rink – and threw it beside the tote.

"Dieter, honey, you can't just go cold turkey. You know that, right?"

"No, I can. I kicked them before. And this time? I got off them early. So it's good."

My sweet lord, he truly believed what he was saying. Oh my…

"Why don't we sit down at that little table on the patio and talk?"

"Sure, yeah, that would be great." He rushed around the bed to the sliding glass doors. Then he threw it open with such eagerness it rattled dangerously when it hit the end of the track. The sounds of Philadelphia floated in. "I'm so glad to see you, Trent. I like you."

"I like you too," I admitted.

I took the tote in hand again, and walked past him and

out onto the cramped patio. The city lay spread out below us, skyscrapers reaching up to touch the setting sun. The table and chairs were dusty. Dieter ran inside when I wrinkled my nose, and returned with a T-shirt to wipe the seats and table with. Then he pulled out my chair as if I were a duchess being seated at a grand ball.

"Thank you," I murmured as I took my seat.

He tossed the dirty shirt into his room then sat down across from me. He looked peaked and tired. I predicted he would look much worse over the next few days if he'd truly dumped all the painkillers. I said nothing, though, just reached into the tote and set small plastic Tupperware dishes on the round glass table. Down below on the street a car alarm pealed, but only for a moment.

"This smells good. What is it?" He'd lifted the lid on the container holding a mountain of pork *kaldereta*.

"It's a dish made with pork and tomatoes. Kind of like pork stew, I guess. My grandmother made it yesterday, but it's better the next day."

"Is your grandmother Japanese or Chinese?" He took the silverware I handed him. "Is that too nosy? I'm just…I want to know about you; your family and stuff."

"No, she's Pilipino. She married my grandfather, an American serviceman, when he was stationed in Manila at Subic Bay during the Vietnam Conflict. She came back with him, had my mother here in the States, and became a citizen back in the seventies."

"Oh, okay, so you're like a quarter Pilipino then."

"Something like that." I opened a smaller dish with some *pandesal* bread left over from breakfast. "And you're German, right? Dieter Lehmann – that sounds *really* German."

"Mmm, yeah, half. My mom's Canadian. She used to figure skate."

"Oh?" I handed him a bit of bread. He grinned and thanked me, then dipped the round roll into his stew.

"Yeah, she's a huge fan of yours. She said she was going to see if my father and her could come down from Canada while we're here filming to maybe meet you."

"That would be nice."

I ripped off a small bit of bread, then reached over to dunk it in his massive container of stew. He nodded and shoved his roll into his mouth. It seemed like the perfect time to push into the addiction talk, but…

If I did, then he'd get upset and this nice moment would be gone. So I let it go for now. We ate and made small talk instead, his eyes never leaving me. I knew I wasn't doing myself or Dieter any favors by backpedaling. I just wanted this peaceful time before I confronted him with the cold, hard facts.

When the food was gone, Dieter sprang up, ran inside, and came out with two bottles of beer. I took mine to be polite.

"Don't you like beer?"

"I do, but it's really fattening." I read the label, rolled my eyes, and took a long pull. Might as well. I'd already eaten two dozen cookies. My ass would be ginormous by the end of the year.

"You're really lean. I don't think a beer now and then is going to hurt you much."

"Well, as you know, empty calories are the devil's play-things for athletes. We could be putting good fuel into our bodies, but this is delicious." I kissed the neck of the dark brown bottle.

Dieter snorted and walked over to the railing. He leaned down to rest his forearms on the wrought-iron rail. He had nice forearms. Thick, lightly haired, powerful. Like the rest of him. I laughed lightly at myself sitting there drinking beer while eye-fucking a hockey player. My, how Trent Hanson's world had changed.

Dieter looked over his shoulder at me. "Something funny?"

I shook my head and stood up to join him at the railing, leaving my beer on the table with the dirty Tupperware containers. He watched me come at him, like a man too stunned to move out of the way of an oncoming steel girder. If truth be told, it was *me* being pulled to *him*. Like a mound of metal shavings to a magnet. I placed my hand on his forearm, the one I'd been admiring from the table. The skin under my palm twitched. His gold-green eyes closed for a second and then reopened, snaring my sight, holding it. I ran my fingers upward, trailing them over the sensitive inner fold of his arm, then sliding them under the sleeve of his dusky blue Railers T-shirt.

"There's nothing funny about this at all, is there?" I asked as my fingers bit into the huge muscle of his biceps.

His head moved back and forth.

My gaze lingered on his mouth. He would taste like beer and spicy pork. It was too much for a man as weak as me. My left hand rose from my side to cup his face. His cheek was thick with new whiskers. The abrasion on my tender palm fired off a jolt of want that raced to my crotch. His eyes were beautiful, entrancing. It was like gazing into the heart of a jungle thick with jade-green plants and brilliant shafts of golden sun.

"You want to go inside? I do. I want to take you to bed."

There was only one way to answer that. I led his mouth to mine with gentle pressure to his jaw. The kiss went from delicate to demanding in the span of a millisecond. His teeth bounced off mine. I slid my hand around his head, dug my fingers deeply into the back of his skull, and speared his mouth with my tongue.

Dieter moaned low and long, meeting me stroke for stroke. Then, as if I'd scripted it from the deep recesses of my favorite fantasies, he straightened, towering over me now, his mouth sealed over mine, and dropped his bottle of beer to the table. It missed. We didn't care. As malt and hops poured over the table and onto the patio, Dieter and I stumbled back inside, pulling at clothing while sucking on each other's mouths. You know, like the "just friends" that we were supposed to be.

EIGHT

Dieter

K issing stopped Trent talking. That was all I thought when I considered kissing him, but the minute our lips touched I went from using a kiss as a distraction to wanting him under me in bed in ten seconds flat.

Even the way Trent wriggled out of his clothes was sexy, and I tried my hardest to be sexy myself, but there was nothing hot in the way I ripped at my clothes and yanked Trent, naked, back onto my bed.

Trent was my new addiction, it seemed, and I needed him as much as I used to need the next opiate hit. I couldn't stop kissing him, and he was so small I could pull him close and support all his weight with mine. He lay sprawled over me, hard against my thigh, and he gripped hard with his hands in my hair. And the kissing…fuck, I wanted all of him; I wanted more, kissing and touching.

Need clawed inside me. "I want to fuck you," I said into his ear, "please."

"Tell me you have stuff," Trent said. Then went back to biting at my neck and kissing his way to my lips.

Blindly, I reached out and slapped my hand on the

bedside cabinet, moving and taking Trent with me when I couldn't reach. He laughed into the kiss, and it was the sweetest but dirtiest laugh I'd ever heard. Between us we found lube, condoms, and my dildo, which for some reason had Trent's eyes widening.

"Tell me you use this on yourself," he said. "Tell me you switch."

I kissed the answer into his heated skin and rolled us so I was on top. "On all fours," I said. I wanted to fuck him face to face, but first I wanted to look; I wanted to know everything about this man. He complied with a grin, spreading himself for me, and I stared.

"You going to do something?" Trent asked, looking at me over his shoulder.

I suited up, grabbed the lube, slicked my fingers, and touched every single inch. His cock was perfect, his ass tight, his thighs – god, his thighs – and I was lost. I traced cold patterns on his skin, concentrating on his cock, back to his balls, slicking his hole with just enough pressure that he was rocking back on my hand. I pressed inside as I bit his ass, then soothed the nip with my tongue. Something knocked my knee, and I glanced down to see the dildo in Trent's hand.

"Stretch me," he demanded.

Fuck, he was demanding, and for a second I imagined him ordering me to my knees, making me suck him off. I groaned at the thought, slicking the dildo and pressing it against him as I kissed his ass, his thighs. I used my weight to push him down so his head was in the pillows and he was supporting his weight on his elbows. Like that I could ease the fat head into him and watch it stretching him, imagining my cock in there. I gripped his cock, slid my hand from root to tip in a shaky rhythm, and the dildo was deeper, and the noises Trent made… They were obscene. Demanding.

Jesus, I was losing it.

I eased the dildo free and slid my cock into its place, smoothly, hesitating only for a moment to check if Trent was okay. But he pushed back – he wanted me inside – and I was ready to do my bit. More than ready.

I caged him under me, resting my forehead on his shoulder, and I wanted more. I wanted to kiss him; I needed to turn him. I moved back, took him with me, resting him on my thighs, fully seated inside him, and he turned his face and I could kiss him. Awkwardly, messily, but they were the best kisses as we groaned into them and demanded everything from each other. I wrapped my hands around his chest, lifted him, helped him up, gasping as he slid back down.

Fuck. I've never…

"Touch yourself," I ordered, and he did as he was told in an instant. I could see his hand on his cock, then taste him in his kisses, and I was so close, but I wanted him to come with me, even given how impossible that could be.

I beat him to it by seconds, forcing myself so deep I worried I'd hurt him, but he joined me, coming and gasping into the kiss. We stayed locked like that for a second, until my knee began to ache and I eased out of him, wiping us with my discarded T-shirt and lying down on the bed. He came right to me, snuggling into my hold and sighing.

"That was good," he murmured. "More than good."

And all I could think was that sex with Trent was the best freaking sex of my entire life so far.

. . .

FEELING sick was what woke me. Trent was still curled against me, his face smooshed into the pillow, his hand on my chest. I eased out from under him, and he muttered something in his sleep but didn't move. I padded to the bathroom, rubbing my belly, thinking back to what I'd eaten.

What if the kaldereta *was laced with something? What if Trent is trying to get me off his skating program?*

I shook my head clear of the stupid and wiped at my brow, which was sweaty, then sat on the side of the bath. The nausea was right there, boiling in my stomach, and I moved to sit next to the toilet, everything I'd eaten that night ending up consigned to the bowl. I didn't think I'd been noisy, had tried to be sick as quietly as I could, but Trent was there, pressing a cool towel to my head and murmuring words that made no sense to me at that moment.

He laid a hand over my chest, right on my heart, and huffed, then helped me to stand. For a slim guy, he was so damn strong. He led me to the bed and urged me to sit down, but I didn't want to sit there – I had this urge to go out to the balcony and sit the fuck still in the night air.

"I need some air," I said, or at least, that was what I wanted to say, politely, but what came out was more of a grunted "fuck you" when Trent attempted to get me to stay in place. There was a silent tussle, but I won – however strong Trent was, I still had fifty pounds on him, and the will of a hockey player who wanted his own way.

The air was cool, and I sank into the chair, kicking away the empty beer bottle and watching it roll to the corner near the door.

When did I drop that? I guarantee some asshole dropped it from another apartment. No sense in wasting good beer. Fuckers.

Trent followed me out, pressed his hand to my heart

again, and I shoved him away, because fuck off with touching me while scowling at me.

"Go away," I snapped. I was embarrassed I'd been sick, my head hurt, and any high from sex had vanished.

"You have any tingling in your arms?" Trent asked, and placed a bottle of water next to me.

I fell on it gratefully, the burn of acid uncomfortable in my throat. It tasted ill; I was ill.

A bug, or goddamn food poisoning. Fucking foreign food.

"No, I don't have any fucking tingling in my arms."

I immediately felt bad. What was wrong with me? Trent was looking after me, giving me water, holding me, cooling my head.

"Your heart is racing," Trent commented, and took the chair next to mine. "Are you anxious?"

Fuck me. "I'm anxious that your grandma's cooking made me sick," I snapped.

Trent simply looked at me, his expression neutral. He looked like he was thinking what to say, and I waited for the words of figure-skater sparkly-assed wisdom.

"You're suffering symptoms of withdrawal," he finally said.

"Whatever," I gave back straight away. Because yeah, that was a sensible response to such a sweeping statement.

"Your heart, being sick, and I bet you're sitting there cursing me for the food, and the care, and the fact that I'm actually witnessing what's happening to you."

"Fuck you, Trent."

He quirked his lips, all disapproving, and shook his head. "Percocet withdrawal isn't life-threatening, it just feels like it," he said, his expression not changing.

"I wasn't using again," I snapped. "My knee hurt, it was pain relief."

"Says the man who took so many tablets he lost his mind."

"It was a mistake, and you know it."

"They weren't even your Percocet," Trent said. He was being so fucking reasonable that my temper was spiraling. "Did you have to buy them off another player, or are they just handed out like sweets between you?"

I didn't answer that. Yes, I'd bought them, a long time ago, back when I'd been in the grip of *real* addiction.

"Mistake or not, you deliberately took more than you should anyway – your downfall was that they were stronger than you were used to."

I wanted to hurt him, wanted to curl my hand into a fist and punch his perfect fucking face.

I don't want to hurt him. He needs to go.

"You can leave," I said. The temper inside me was making me irrational.

He shook his head, seeming determined to pick at the scab that hid my past.

"When did you take the last pill?"

"I didn't," I said, and I sure as hell knew I was being irrational. Didn't what? What was I even denying anymore?

Trent worried his lip, and his chocolate eyes were bright, like he was trying not to cry. What the hell? Why was he crying?

"However long it's been, about seventy-two hours after that last dose, symptoms of withdrawal tend to peak – severe, intense. It's only going to get worse. You understand that, right?"

He sounded like he was reading from a technical manual, and believe me, I'd read them all.

I wanted to say something clever about how Trent was overreacting and how I was fine, but all I could think of was to tell him to go, with added expletives. The anger inside me was making it impossible to form a coherent sentence.

He stood. "I don't expect you'll be in tomorrow. I'll tell the team you have food poisoning or something."

Wait. No. "I've never missed a game, or an appearance, I'll be there."

I rubbed my arms. Abruptly I was chilled, even though my head was burning, and nausea threatened again.

"Withdrawal starts when your body expects its next dose," Trent said. "Remember that. You need to get some help with this."

"I don't need anyone else's help."

"You do," he insisted. "You're an addict and you're in denial about having relapsed. Do you have a sponsor?"

Mike was my sponsor, a quiet librarian from my hometown. Not even an NHLer, just some guy who talked sense and was always there for me. I didn't need him; he was part of my past.

"I can't do this with you," Trent murmured when I didn't answer.

He'd decided my addiction was too much for him? Well, whatever. It wasn't like I needed him in my life, with his glittery shit and his figure skating.

But wait. What if I was losing the chance of being with the only man who'd made me think I wanted more? I wanted his brightness in my life. I wanted the glitter and the smile and the fun, and the taste of him, and the flirting and sex.

Great. Now I was going through the pathetic post-sick stage of this whole shitfest. This was all Trent's fault.

Why am I doing this? What's wrong with me? Why is Trent giving up on me after one fuck?

Trent pushed his hands into the pockets of the robe he

was using, my robe. It swamped him. I looked down. I was naked. Sitting on my balcony, balls naked.

And hot.

And cold.

Abruptly, the anger subsided, and I felt pathetic and stupid, and Trent was leaving.

"Please don't go," I said, and I could hear how pathetic I sounded, how needy. What did Trent owe me? Nothing.

"I wish I could stay," he said, but the tone he used told me he was lying. "But it's late and I need to get up early and face another battle."

I held out a hand. "Please stay." I sounded broken and pathetic and all the things that the tablets stopped.

Trent sighed, crossed back to me and sat on the edge of the other chair, taking my hand in his. I loved the way he held my hand, and affection swelled inside me. He understood. He wasn't leaving; he was going to be my friend, my lover, my support. He half smiled at me, and I knew everything would be okay; I hadn't fucked up too bad.

And then he ruined it all.

"Dieter, there's an NHL substances program," he said. "They have counseling as well so I assume you've been in contact with them. Don't they want to see you every so often? You could call them."

What? I yanked away my hand. "Fuck you," I snarled.

"Dieter, if you don't call them…"

"What? You will? You'll fuck up my career because of one lousy misstep?"

"It isn't one, you know that."

"Just fucking go. I don't need your shit, however good of a fuck you are."

He nodded, stood, and left.

And I sat naked on my balcony feeling like everything was going wrong.

I WOKE up still naked on the balcony, to the early light of a Philadelphia day. Feeling like shit. Trent had seen me at my worst and he'd left. Just up and left.

I didn't need him anyway. I was in the NHL now, and there were any amount of puck bunnies out there who wanted me. Hell, one gay club and they'd be all falling over the muscled guy with the contract.

I was the man.

A broken man.

I stumbled back into the bedroom, stopping just inside and turning back to pick up the beer bottle, dropping it in the trash. I made my bed, or at least tried, pulling the covers straight, and sat heavily when I spotted the bright blue of the scarf Trent had been wearing when he'd arrived. I picked up the soft fabric and instinctively buried my nose in it, the scent of my lover just as I remembered.

Lover? No, one-night stand I'd completely fucked things up with.

I picked up my cell, pulling out the charger and thumbing through my contacts. First name I considered connecting to was Layton, telling him to spin something to the team about why I wasn't in today. Then I'd have to be honest about what I was in the middle of right now, and he already had the whole mess of a possible sex tape, and blackmail, although that had been very quiet since that text from Marianna.

The next name on my list was Mike, a number I hadn't used in a long time. I keyed it in before I'd even really thought about it. I hadn't considered time differences, and

I almost hung up on my old sponsor. The one who'd held my hand through some bad times.

Then he answered, his voice sleep-rough and slightly unfocused.

"Dieter?" Mike said my name, just my name. No hello or how are you? I hadn't spoken to him for over a year, and even though he'd called and left me a couple of messages, I hadn't *needed* him. Or at least I hadn't felt like I needed him.

"Mike," I responded, because I didn't know what the hell to say.

There was silence. Not unusual – my conversations with Mike had often included silences where we just sat and thought on opposite ends of the line. I heard movement, the soft exhalation of Mike getting up and out of bed.

"I'll put the coffee on," he murmured.

I did the same, putting him on speaker phone because I needed some distance from the man who'd been my confidant and support for a long time.

I had coffee, I felt sick, my chest tight with anxiety, and coldly I knew this was withdrawal, and that one tablet would ease the pain and confusion.

But Trent said I needed help.

I hated him for that, but I'd made the call to my sponsor, hadn't I?

"I saw you got a contract for a year with the Railers," Mike said, starting the way we used to, exchanging news. I'd received invites to meet up with him and I'd known I really should make the effort, but when I'd been meds-free I hadn't wanted to connect with him again. I'd wanted to consign him to my past.

He would never be part of my past. He would be my everyday support if I needed him.

My friend with all the messy parts included.

"It's a good contract," I said.

"You've worked hard for it," Mike agreed.

"I'm fucking it all up." That pretty much summed it up. "I'm a grinder, I'm not ready for the NHL, my knee hurts all the fucking time, and I don't think I can do it."

Silence again. He was waiting for me to expand, but I didn't know what to say or how to explain it. I needed him to ask me the right questions. I wasn't ready to talk, and I closed my eyes and hoped he would understand.

"Mike, please help me."

NINE

Trent

T o be honest, I don't remember much of the ride home. It was chilly for the middle of summer. My throat and neck were the coldest, because my scarf was still lying beside Dieter's bed. You know, the bed on which I'd spread myself out like an Easter all-you-can-eat buffet. The bed of the man I was supposed to be "only friends" with, yet had allowed to fuck me into a near orgasmic coma with a dildo *and* his dick, because obviously just the man's fat cock wasn't *quite* enough fuckery. What the shit was my problem? Why had I given in to lust so easily? That was not the behavior of a friend trying to help another friend.

"You're a slut, Trent. Oh yes you are. *What are you looking at?!*" I snapped at a man tossing newspapers out of the back of a red van. He flipped me off, and rightfully so.

My scooter tires grabbed some pavement and actually squealed a bit as I flew through a yellow light. My neck was painfully cold. I wished I had my scarf. Admittedly, it was probably only seventy degrees with a light summer breeze, but when one has a cold and shamed soul, one's neck gets frosty.

I pulled up to my mother's house. The front tire bumped the curb, because I was so sick and upset and disgusted with myself that my mind was elsewhere. The scooter tipped and we both fell sideways onto the sidewalk.

With the dawn of another new day tickling the sky with salmon, lilac and cyan, I lay there beside my yellow scooter and stared at the sky, tears leaking from my eyes and streaming into my ears.

What are you doing with your life, Trent? How did the world's premier men's figure-skating star end up sprawled on the sidewalk in front of his mother's house weeping like a kid who's just skinned his knee?

I sat up, tugged off my safflower helmet, and pushed the tips of my cold fingers into my eyes. I had to get my shit together. I sniffled and coughed, wiped my sleeve under my running nose, and slowly got to my feet. When I turned, helmet in hand, my mother was coming down the short walk, her face set and lined

"How many times do I have to tell you to get rid of that damn scooter?!" Her voice was far louder than it should be at this time of the morning. "Are you okay?"

"Like you really care," I snarled.

How dare she come out here in her summer robe and get in my face? I stormed around her, intent on taking this indoors so everyone who lived on 16th Street didn't hear our discussion. She grabbed my arm as I passed. I flew around to face her. Her brown eyes flared and she took a step in reverse, her hand falling to her side.

"Do not do that!" I yelled, and whipped my helmet into the neighbor's yard. It landed on their rhododendrons. "Don't grab me. Not ever! Don't pretend that you give two shits about me."

She opened her mouth to reply. I barreled over her, the only sounds on our street the hum of the streetlights, the flitter of a million moths against glass bulbs, and the reverberation of my shouts bouncing off the small, cramped row houses.

"You went to see him. Why? After all he did to us, to me, your only son, you took a day off work to see Clay."

"Trent…"

"I *begged* you to come spend a day with me at the rink, to be on this miserable fucking show that I'm doing only because it will keep a roof over *your* head!" I inhaled deeply and rolled on, not allowing her any chance to reply. She had hurt me. Badly. And I'd hurt Dieter. And Dieter was hurting himself. So much hurting. We were all drowning in hurt.

"Trent, I just— It's not that I didn't want to see you on the show." She pulled the collar of her robe tighter around her throat. Must be her neck was cold with shame too. "I was too embarrassed to be on it. I married Clay. It's my fault that you're broke now and whoring yourself out to keep me and your *Lola* cared for."

Wonderful. So my mother agreed that I was a slutty whore. This day was just getting better and better, and it wasn't even six a.m. yet.

"Tell me why, then. Make me understand why you chose him over me." I waved my hands around in the air. Her eyes darted around trying to follow them. A light came on across the street in Mr. Cho's bedroom window. "Make me understand why you can't give your son an hour or two to be on his show but you can drive up to Mercer and saunter into the State Correctional Institute and not be ashamed." Words were pouring out of me. I felt lightheaded, and wondered if I was taking time to breathe as I berated my mother. "You could go see the man who stole all my money and gambled it away on dogs, but Trent gets nothing! How can you do that? How the *fuck* can you pick that miserable human being over me?"

"I didn't! I went to see him because I love him, Trent!" Her shouts bounced off the sides of the low-income homes. A few more lights flickered on inside our neighbor's houses.

"Love him?" I blinked at her. "How can you love a man who leaves you broken and starving? Who stole all your son's money and bought booze and other women with it – whatever he didn't drop on the fucking greyhounds, that is. How can you possibly love someone like Clay?"

"He has addictions, Trent." Now she sounded weak, teary, just like she always did when confronted with her choice of men. "He asked about you. He wants to see you…to talk."

"Then why the hell would you be with him?" I refused to comment on the whole Clay wanting to see me comment. Hell would freeze over before *that* happened.

"Because I love him!"

"Only idiots love people with addictions!" I roared. My words echoed back at me, resonating off the front of Mr. Cho's battered brick row house. I slapped my hands over my mouth. What had I just said? *What had I just said?*

"Trent, you don't mean that. You loved Jonah so much…"

She took a step toward me. I stumbled in reverse, shaking my head violently. "He never loved me," I coughed into my palms. "He couldn't, because he loved the dope more. Same as Dieter." I dropped into a crouch, resting my back against the cheap fencing that ran around the postage-stamp-sized yard.

"Dieter? Who's Dieter?" Mom asked.

I ignored her and just cried. For so long that 16th Street was waking up in earnest before I got myself together enough to go to the rink, my mother begging and pleading with me to come inside and talk more. There were no more words or emotions in me, so I righted my scooter and took off, leaving my helmet on Mrs. Patel's pink rhododendrons. Who cared if I T-boned a car without my skid lid? Not Jonah. Not my mother. Not Clay. Not my father, who got himself killed before I could even talk. And certainly not Dieter.

Rainbow Skate appeared mysteriously in front of me. Had I crossed the city already? Huh. I'd wept and scooted all the way there without kissing a phone pole or the back of a Subaru, so yay me. First stop once inside the empty rink was a bathroom. I looked at myself and wanted to weep again. My hair was a windblown, sexed-up mess. My eyes were puffy and red, my cheeks splotchy, and my neck bore a brilliant purple hickey the size of my thumb.

"This right here is a complete mess," I muttered.

I turned on the cold water and patted down my cheeks and hair, to no avail. Knowing it was beyond a sink bath, I went to the showers and stood under the hot water, lost as a man could be, soaping my ass and wincing at the reminder of being loved by a hockey player on the edge. I had to put on my dirty clothes. I skipped the day-old briefs and threw them in the trash. Then I went to the manager's office, sat behind Dan's desk, and pretended to work. Work consisted of staring at Dieter on a continual loop of video.

What was I doing allowing myself to fall into this kind of relationship again? I turned off the tapes of Dieter Lehmann and let my eyes drift shut. I had a couple of hours before the Railers and the fucking cameras would show up. I'd push through the training today, make my calls to the charity event I'd missed in order to tumble into Dieter's bed, then go home to my place and sew. Or eat tubs of frozen whipped topping while watching *Steel Magno-*

lias and wallowing in self-pity and disgrace. Or I could get drunk. Either would work.

I'd been asleep for only a short while when a thunderous rap on the open door jarred me awake. Heart in throat, I found Stan filling the doorway of Dan's small office.

"We work me good." He folded his arms over his massive chest after ducking to enter the

room. I scrubbed at my face with my hands. He smelled of coffee and doughnuts. My stomach rumbled but there was no way I was feeding it.

"You hungry. Should eat."

"I'm not eating today. I've stuffed enough food into me the past couple of weeks to sink a tubby old ship."

His gray eyes narrowed a bit, not so much in anger but in concern.

"I need to abstain a bit. Maybe just do a liquid diet. I'll be fine." I found my Superstar Trent smile and glued it into place.

"You eat. Not eating is bad."

"Not when you're a fatty potato like I am." I patted my flat stomach, then slowly pushed out of the creaky chair. Or were those sounds coming from my stiff back? "Let me get some coffee and we'll—"

"No. We eat now. Skate needs food. Mm-Mm good."

"Soup? We're having soup for breakfast?"

He nodded, then took me by the wrist and led me to the row of vending machines. I peeked up at the huge man. Stan smiled down, then waved a hand the size of a hubcap at the machines.

"Eat Mm-Mm soup. Drink milk. Make energy for skating. I wait."

"*Fine.*" I sighed and fed some money into the damn machines.

When I had soup and a container of two percent milk, my diet guru and I went back to Dan's office. I ate. Stan sat across from me, all eighteen feet of him folded into a puny chair, talking away as I sipped on my chicken rice. It tasted rather good.

"I keep eye on food for you like Layton."

"Okay." I spooned in some rice and broth. It slid down my tender throat. Crying for hours on end is tough on a soul. "Do you think I'm being a twat?"

"What is twat?" He tried to sit back and get comfortable, but his frame was just too long and gangly for comfort in that chair.

"Oh, uh, it's a word for a lady's feminine region."

"Ah, yes. Feminine freshness."

I coughed on my sip of soup. "If you insist. I've never been close enough to a feminine region to say if they're fresh or not. I like the boys far too much."

Stan smiled. It was a kind smile that crinkled the skin around his pretty eyes and changed him from Mr. Intimidating to Mr. Cutie-Pie.

"You love Dieter like Tennant loves Jared. I see you and him making google eyes. Is good."

Thank the gods my little Styrofoam cup of soup was empty. It slid from my fingers and landed on my lap. I stared openly at the goalie.

"No, no, no," I said while fishing the cup from between my legs. "Love has not been mentioned. Not once. It was merely sex. Great sex, yes, but just sex. I can't love a man like him. Never again. It hurts too much. Better to walk away now before we both end up being more crushed."

Where the shit had my spoon gone?

"Never walk away from man you love."

My eyes lifted from my soup search to find his. Lovely,

they were – big and gray with dark lashes and topped with incredibly expressive brows. And sad. So incredibly sad.

"Sometimes walking away is for the best."

He shook his head. "Is never best. Come." He shoved to his feet. "Let us work on speed."

I sat there with my cup *sans* spoon and watched him leave, his broad shoulders sliding through the door on an angle.

Stan and I got an hour alone on the ice. He was coming along nicely. He'd never have the speed that the smaller players had, but he was quicker on his skates now. His height was considered an advantage, or so I'd been told, in that he filled up more of the net, making it harder for the other team to score. He was pleasant to work with. The big man smiled most of the time, tried to tell jokes but always fouled up the punchline, and worked like a dog to implement all that I was trying to pass along.

Then the cameras arrived. And the makeup people, and the producer, and the sound men. Stan nodded and chatted. I sulked and bitched. So much, in fact, that my agent was called out by the show producer, a short round man named Kurt who was very nice, I was sure, when he wasn't being a feminine region that starts with C.

Gayle found me sitting in the top row of red seats, my hands under my armpits and my skates resting on the back of the seat in front of me. She climbed up the twenty rows and flopped down beside me, her gloved hands holding two large cups of hot drink.

"Hot chocolate," she said, then pushed the extra-large cup of calories at me.

I waved it away with my elbow and a sour look. "I'm fasting for the rest of the day."

"Ah, well this isn't food – it's drink."

She lifted the edge of the cup and blew a steamy cloud of cocoa goodness into my face.

"Cow-bag," I huffed, then took the drink from her.

She smiled, and we sat side by side sipping for a few moments. The Railers and the production crew were milling around on the ice. I took note of the fact that Dieter was not among the men in dusky blue jerseys, and my heart grew more dejected.

"Would you like to tell me why you're refusing to go on camera today?"

"I'm having personal issues," I mumbled into my cup.

"What kind of personal issues?"

"Personal ones."

"That's not helpful, Trent," she said with a touch of schoolmarm in her voice.

I cocked an eyebrow and took a drink. It was sinfully sweet.

"You know you signed a contract to deliver so many hours of film. If you start pulling back, they're going to start getting crabby. Honey, you can't afford a lawsuit for breach of contract."

"Let them sue me. I'm a vile person who says vile things about people who are struggling."

"Trent, you're not a vile person." She sounded tired.

Well, such was the life of anyone who got near me. I tired people out. Just ask my choreographer. She would attest to how tiresome Trent Hanson was. She was probably dancing in the streets knowing she wouldn't have to put up with me anymore.

"You're a wonderful person," Gayle said.

"Pfft. You should have heard me around five this morning. You'd change your mind about my wonderful status."

I lifted my right hand from my cup to rest it on my throat. It was still cold.

"Trent, you *have* to perform today for those cameras. I'm not sure what happened off-ice, but you know better than anyone that athletes can't let what happens in their personal lives affect them on the field…or ice, as the case may be."

"I'm not a skater anymore…"

"Tell that to the kids who idolize you," she said softly. A tiny marshmallow stuck in my throat.

"You're a terribly shitty woman to say that to me," I snapped.

Gayle patted my thigh, then got to her feet.

"I just want…"

"What do you want?"

I searched among the hockey players, and when my eyes couldn't find him, I knew what I wanted. I just wasn't sure I had the guts to be with him.

"I want courage."

"I've never seen a man with more bravery than you have." She smiled at me, then went back to the ice. Her hand-knitted hat was atrocious, but in a way that made it cute. Not fashionable, no – far from it – but cute. Like a soccer mom kind of cute.

I sat there and drank my hot chocolate. All the while I thought of Jonah and Dieter, of my mother and Clay, of my grandmother, of this rink and those cameras and the men on the ice and the kids in school. My kids. They needed me to do this. My mother and *Lola* needed me to do this. Dieter needed me to do this. *I* needed me to do this.

"Okay, the chocolate has made me feel *all* better! Let's make some reality TV!" I shouted from the rafters, my smile firmly in place. I hoped the makeup man had good foundation. My face and neck were a wreck, as was my life.

But at least I wasn't walking away from this or from Dieter. Stan would be thrilled.

TEN

Dieter

If anyone was looking for me, they would see I was there. Up in the gods, three rows from the back in the nosebleed chairs, looking down at the men on the ice. Watching them and wishing I were down there with them.

I'd missed three sessions now, but none of this was obligatory; no one was on my ass demanding that I attend. But I wanted so much to be learning more. I was missing out, because every one of us who'd listened to Trent was faster, more focused, and I was stuck now.

And not just because of the shit that had gone down with the tablets, no – this was about the fact that I was there for results on my knee, and I knew they wouldn't be good. The only thing keeping me on the ice had been painkillers, and look where that had gotten me.

I was losing my last chance to get an NHL spot; the Railers would take one look at me, my knee, my stupid fucking addictions, and I would be gone.

They were a progressive team, focused on inclusion and fairness and all kinds of things PC, but even they couldn't carry a skater who couldn't skate on the roster.

On the ice, the guys were working on glides again, and even from up here I could see the improvements. Stan was on one side talking to Trent, and my chest tightened when he lifted a wriggling Trent and held him up in a parody of a lift. He soon set him down, but the damage was done; I'd seen Trent laughing, enjoying his time with the team.

And I wasn't there.

Trent's work might prove to give us an edge as a team, just that small difference to push us one more round in the playoffs.

Us? There wouldn't be an us. I was looking at injured reserve, or even worse.

The session finished, and I slid down in my chair, pulling my ball cap low over my face, hidden up in the shadows where no one would think to look. This place was no East River Arena, only thirty or so rows of seats, but I was far enough away to hide for sure.

When the rink was empty, I left my seat, heading for the exit to the parking lot before anyone noticed me.

"I saw you," Trent said from behind me.

I turned to face him, carefully because I felt like shit, and my knee hurt, and I was done with today.

"Hey," I said, which was all I could manage.

Trent looked tired but good. His eyes were smudged with kohl, his hair artfully tousled and streaked with what looked like a jade green in this light. He was all in black, his familiar diamanté piping around his collar, and he looked so good.

And I had fucked up; thrown it all away.

"You should come down on the ice with us," Trent said when I stood there looking at him blankly.

"I have to get back to Harrisburg today. I have..." I waved at my knee, then up at my head, like that explained everything. I didn't expect him to understand. "I'm sorry," I blurted out, with no framework for what exactly I was apologizing for.

He smiled at me – not a huge smile, more sad than happy, but it was a beautiful smile, and abruptly I needed to touch him. I stepped into his space and cradled his face in my hands, tilting his head to mine.

"I'm so sorry," I repeated.

"I know you are," he murmured. There was none of his usual sass, there was no fire in his eyes. All I saw was sadness. I leaned down and pressed a kiss to his lips. Just one, and then I left without looking back at him.

Maybe he'd still be there for me after I was done with whatever I had to do next.

Maybe he wouldn't.

I just had to have hope, because somehow, in a short space of time, Trent had become the center of everything for me.

Everything.

MY PHONE VIBRATED to remind me of the need to get my ass in gear and to the airport for my flight back to Harrisburg. The flight itself was short, the cab ride from the airport to the arena even shorter, giving me no time to get my head in a good place.

Grief took my breath as I walked into the East River Arena, under the banners with pictures of the team. I saw numbers and photos of Connor, Stan, Ten, Arvy, but none of me yet.

I suspected I would never make it up there. The shop held my jersey with my number and name on the back, but I doubted that anyone would buy it.

Idly, I wondered how many they'd brought in for my fans, and I couldn't help the snort of derision that I even had fans.

Jeez, I have it bad today.

I slipped into one of the many small rooms off the main corridor, and took a moment to settle my thoughts. I couldn't go into this meeting feeling like I was already done. I had to channel some kind of courage from somewhere, and lace it tight with hope. It took me a while to get my breathing settled, even longer to find that kernel of courage that I had to dig really deep for, but finally I was as ready as I would ever be, and I moved out of the shadow and into the brightly lit corridor.

When I knocked on the doc's door, I was exactly on time, and I heard the gruff, "Come in." He stood as I entered, extending his hand and saying something generic. I wasn't sure what, because I was looking at his face, judging his expression, trying to see any microscopic changes that might indicate how bad the news could be. I wanted him to give me the news in words of one syllable, no fancy explanations. Was I done? What was wrong with me that PT and manipulation couldn't help with?

"How have you been?" Doc asked, and I stared at him blankly.

"I'm good," I said. Because what I really wanted to say would have the Doc consigning me to anger management and counseling all in one go.

He gestured to the X-rays up on the backlit boards, and encouraged me to stand closer, and then he began, with words that meant nothing. He wrote down what was wrong with me, and I read it to myself as he explained. Sporadic osteochondritis dissecans. That was what made my knee joint snap and swell and throw me off stride. That long name meant I needed surgery.

"It's probably been caused by injury, but it could also be due to repetitive use of the joint."

Repetitive use? Hockey players – hell, any kind of professional sports person – knew what repetitive use was all about. It was how we trained muscle memory.

He pointed at the X-ray, and I peered at what he was trying to show me. "The knee is a synovial joint where three bones articulate with each other – the femur, tibia and patella – and has two articulations."

I must have looked at him blankly, because he frowned and repeated that again. This time I nodded to indicate that I understood. Of course I understood. I knew my knee intimately; each muscle, tendon and bone when I pressed and pushed to get the pain to go.

He continued, and I tried to look like I understood so he didn't repeat himself. I didn't want to hear this, I wanted a conclusion.

"The articular bones are covered by white, shiny and elastic cartilage, and the smooth articular surface of the femur, here." He tapped the X-ray with a pen. "That rolls and slides on the tibia plateau, with synovial fluid that nourishes and lubricates the cartilage."

"And?"

Please cut to the chase. My head hurts, my stomach is a mess, and I need to get out of here to my next meeting – the important one where I tell management what a fucking mess of a skater they contracted.

"In patients with osteochondritis dissecans, the subchondral bone with its articular cartilage doesn't get any blood supply anymore, and degenerates. Luckily, you're at stage three with some partially detached lesions – what we call a dissecans 'in situ'."

"I'm lucky. Does that mean some rest and PT and I'm okay to play?"

Doc looked right at me. He was an expert in being straight with players, renowned for it on the team. "No, Dieter, I'm sorry. You will need an operation. We would look to repair the blood supply by inserting an arthroscope through the cartilage and the site of the osteochondrosis into the healthy bones, then stabilizing the fragment by pinning or with screw fixation. Look, I know this is a lot to take in, but the operation itself is a simple one, and you would need six to ten weeks of recovery and physical therapy, then you could be back on the ice."

I did a quick calculation in my head. Six weeks was right at the start of the season, ten weeks meant I'd miss games, sidelined. The Railers had pulled me from the farm team to play, not sit in the owner's box looking down on games.

I was fucked.

"What if I don't have the operation?"

Doc didn't react like a normal doctor would. He didn't look shocked or concerned – hell, he dealt with skaters who demanded to play even with broken legs or shattered eye sockets. He was used to the idiocy and bravado of the hockey player.

"That is your choice, of course," he began carefully, "but my report to management with the advice for you to have an operation is the foundation for your inclusion in the roster. They will insist you get the work done, because you'd be no good to them otherwise." He softened a little now he'd delivered his advice about what the team would want me to do. "Also, Dieter, the pain you must be in at times...we need to stop that for you, okay?"

I nodded, because I think he expected me to understand that last part.

"Now, we can have you in the hospital tomorrow. You'd

be back and resting in a couple of days, rehabbing within a few weeks. Shall I set it up?"

He was asking me the question, looking at me for an answer, and I'd lost my words, all the words. I had nothing.

So I nodded mutely, and my chest hurt, and I felt sick, and the walls of the doc's office were closing in on me.

He pressed a hand to my shoulder. "Let's move this up to the meeting with management, okay?"

I followed him out of the office to the elevator that would take us the four floors to the team admin area, where management rubbed shoulders with marketing, and where the decision would be made to void my contract. Once they found out about the opiates, about my addiction…

I would be gone.

Everyone was there. Felix Cote, the owner; Dawson Brown, the manager; the player rep, Anatoly 'Toly' Sokolov, a ten-year veteran who worked hard for the team; and Coach Benning. Connor Hurleigh, captain of the Railers, was there as well. I thought he'd have been in Philly with Trent and the rest, but come to think of it, I hadn't seen him on the ice that morning. He threw me a smile and stood up to fist-bump me. I liked Connor. He was a good guy, a good player…hell, he was one hundred percent made of good.

I'd bet he never took Percocet to chase a high.

Doc settled on one of the array of sofas and so did the others, so I took my own seat and waited for the sentence.

"What we're looking at is potentially having you on injured reserve for the start of the season, aiming to get you back on the ice for November – at least that's our understanding from what Doc has explained." Cote cut straight to the chase without any talk about the injury or how it might have happened. He wouldn't care how, just about the mechanics of getting me on the ice. "You'll travel with the team, and we'll press-release a lower-body injury. How does that sound?"

To a normal man, one who had a fucked up knee, one who wasn't battling addictions, that would sound fine; a solid plan.

Doc was talking to Coach, Connor leaned in listening, about rehab, and PT, and I was abruptly not even present in the room. I was a chess piece they were positioning, with plans in place to have me rehabbing, back playing November.

"I have something I want to say," I said, but no one stopped talking. "Please," I said a little louder, and one by one they looked at me. "I have something to say."

I stared right at Connor and Toly. They were possibly the only ones in the room who would truly understand addiction in a player, or the need for pain relief that became more. They would have seen it on so many levels.

"I'm an addict," I began, and swallowed, my mouth dry. "I'm addicted to opiates, and while I had everything under control before – attending sessions, having a sponsor – I didn't tell anyone on the team or my agent." I lied about that, because even though he'd dumped my ass, Bob was a good guy; I wasn't going to throw him under the bus. "I relapsed when the pain became too bad in the playoffs, and I need help."

There. I'd said it. I didn't have to add that I understood if they wanted me off the team – that was a given. There were ECHL teams out there who would be happy to have me play despite my shit, so I wouldn't have to give up.

I just wouldn't be there with the Railers.

"Ahh," Cote said, and sat back at his desk, resting his hands on his soft belly, courtesy of one too many social occasions in the name of the Railers, I should imagine. He wasn't an ex-skater, he was a money guy who loved hockey. He couldn't know what it was like to drag yourself onto the ice with an injury.

"Toly?" Connor asked our teammate, the players' rep, the one whose job it was to look out for me. I'd blindsided him as well; it wasn't as if I'd told him what was happening. The only one I'd told was Layton.

I should have told more people.

Toly was still staring at me, but not in a way that worried me. He didn't look pissed that this was the first he'd heard of it, any more than Connor did. A rush of thankfulness made me lightheaded, and I must have done something good in a previous life not to get a fist in the face from either of them.

"This is first I heard," Toly began, his Russian accent sexy and low. "I will work with Dieter."

"I will as well," Connor said, and I realized how pathetically grateful I was to have Connor as my captain. The man was quiet but fair, and he didn't have a bad bone in his body. "I'm concerned how this will impact the team, but for now let's take this a step at a time."

Cote nodded. "We'll get Layton on this," he announced.

Poor Layton; he was getting all the team shit to deal with.

"Okay," Cote finally said, "you'll make contact with the substance abuse program, work on that alongside rehab. It won't be easy, but I've seen players get through this before. I won't say I'm happy about the situation, but you have the Railers' support to get you back on the ice where we want to see you." He leaned forward again and looked right at me. "You belong in this team, Dieter, but make no mistake – if you can't crack this, we will have to come up with a plan B."

"I understand."

I was still looking at Connor, because the player in me needed the reassurance – hell, the approval of my captain. He still didn't look pissed; equally, he didn't look like he was throwing his arms out for a life-affirming bro-hug.

But he wasn't shocked. I could work with that.

Then he nodded. "We'll get through this together," he said. He didn't mean he'd be holding my hand through therapy and the operation, he just meant he had my back.

And now I felt like I wanted to fucking cry.

Cote cleared his throat. "We'll do a press release about the LBI, state that you'll be out for the start of the season. Doc here can feedback on progress, and you'll refer yourself, with our support, to the substance abuse program and get clear and cohesive SAP counseling."

My stomach sank. I'd expected that; they were investing in me, and they knew that the SAP was the best system for me to get my head right.

"You're voluntarily making contact, and you will rehab and have counseling, and we'll take a view…" He looked at the pad on his lap. "Mid-September."

There was nothing I could say to any of that. They were right. If I wanted the NHL, I had to do what I was told, and they hadn't taken away my chance of being a Railer.

I just had to prove to them they were right not to give up on me.

But while I sat there scared shitless, with the dark tunnel of pain and rehab ahead of me, I just wanted two things.

I wanted a Percocet to take the edge off.

And I wanted Trent to still want me even though I was fucked.

. . .

WHEN I WAS BACK in my apartment, I wrote a long text to Trent, my thoughts and hopes, and the fact that I wanted him to talk to me and be there for me and about how sorry I was that I'd messed up.

Then I backspaced it all and sent just two words.

It's done.

ELEVEN

Trent

———————

"He sent me a text that said, 'It's done'. Just that. Just those two words. What the flying fuck does that mean? Is he in rehab? In the hospital? Hockey players," I huffed, and gave the ceiling of my rink a sour look as I kept talking. "So I called Adler Lockhart, who tells me that he's having surgery. Which is good, he needs to attend to his knee, but what about the pain afterward? He looked sober when he was here yesterday, but…well, yeah, *but*. And now I'm even more lost and confused because every damn fiber of my being is screaming for me to go to Harrisburg and see him, you know?"

The Tennant Rowe bobblehead that Layton and the Railers had presented me with bobbled its head in reply. Wonderful. *So* helpful. I should shove it back in its box.

"Do you think I should?" I lifted the tiny resin figure from my lap and shook it. It just bobbled, as any good bobblehead should. I sighed and set it down on the cold, plastic seat beside me, right next to the check I'd also gotten from the Harrisburg Railers in attendance. The players who'd come to this debacle of a training session/reality show had handed me a personal check for ten thousand dollars for the rink. The real Tennant Rowe had tried to put the check into my palm just two hours ago, before they'd left to return to their lives for the rest of the summer.

"What you're doing here is important," he'd said as I tried gracefully not to take their money.

"Showing a bunch of orangutans how to shave a few milliseconds off their time?"

The group gathered around me chuckled.

"No, what you're doing with the kids. Giving them a haven, a place to train without being judged or hated on. *That's* the important thing." He pressed the check into my chest. And held it there, right over my fluttering heart. How had I gotten so attached to this pod of apes so quickly? They'd certainly showed me that not all hockey players were lumbering cretins bent on humiliating the little figure skater with the perfectly applied eyeliner and gloss. Imagine that. Giving people a chance and not judging on past experiences. What a novel concept.

"And turning us all on to Pilipino food," Arvy chimed in.

"Good Pilipino food," Stan enthused. Another round of laughter.

"I'll be happy to take this for the children. Thank you." I hugged Rowe and Jared, then went down the line, giving each of them a hug and a soft kiss on the lips. Not a sexual kiss, just a friendly one. The sexual kisses were reserved for the Railer who wasn't there. "Now get your fine asses back to Harrisburg or wherever it is hockey players go when there's no hockey."

"Home," Layton said, taking a moment to shake my hand then press a bobblehead into it.

"We're all going home. Please, if you're ever in the

capital, give us a call and come see a game. I'll make sure you have tickets waiting at the will call window."

"Oh, yes, of course. If I'm ever in Harrisburg, I will."

"And thank you for keeping our secret," Adler whispered by my ear.

I waved that off with a sweep of a hand.

Then, *en masse*, they'd left. And Rainbow Skate had seemed so much larger, and far too still. I'd taken a seat right by the ice and had a long conversation with bobbly Tennant Rowe. Which had really gotten me nowhere. My head was still a quagmire of fear and doubt and anger. I hadn't spoken to my mother yet. I was too hurt to take her calls. I'd hardly slept last night, tossing and turning, checking for texts from Dieter. I would look like a haggard pile of horse manure when I had to go out on the town with that miserable camera crew this evening.

They wanted me to cruise the clubs in the Gayborhood, a lovely and festive part of town known for its fabulousness and rich gay lifestyle, stores, and nightclubs. They wanted me to flirt, giggle, tease; sprinkle the world with glitter, light, and homosexuality. Be Trent Hanson. But Trent Hanson didn't want to cruise the clubs and preen for the cameras or the men who would flock to him. He just wanted to be left alone to figure out what he was doing with his life. And why he seemed drawn to men who were living their lives in utter chaos.

"Do you think I need counseling as well?" I asked resin Tennant. His head wobbled around. "Is that a yes or a no? You need to be more decisive. Those good looks will only get you so far, you know."

"Trent?"

I started violently, nearly dropping Tennant to the cold cement. To my immediate right stood Pearl Denning and Scotty, my brave and brilliant student who was the only openly trans child in the ranks. Scotty held a huge part of my heart.

I looked at the watch buried among several bangles on my wrist. "You're here early," I said, getting my professional Trent persona quickly in place. "Our private session isn't until ten."

Mrs. Denning's face was tight and lined with sadness. Scotty, who always smiled, was hiding inside her hoodie, one of a hundred she owned that had little Scottish Terriers on it. Everything she owned, it seemed, had tiny black dogs on it. It was so her.

"There was an incident at school, and Scotty wanted to come early so she could talk to you about it. She won't talk to anyone else."

"Well then, why don't we sit down here and talk." I patted the seat on my right.

Mrs. Denning looked close to tears. She whispered, "Thank you", then pressed a kiss to the top of her child's red hoodie. She left us to talk. Scotty sat on the edge of her seat, her white figure skates dangling off a lean shoulder, long black hair escaping her hood.

"Bad day at school?" I asked after a few moments of uncomfortable silence had passed.

Scotty nodded.

"Did someone make fun of you for dressing like a girl?"

Scotty nodded.

"That's hurts, doesn't it?"

Scotty nodded.

I wiggled up to the edge of my seat and crossed one leg over the other. Then I leaned further forward to peer into that dark hood of hers. "Did you know that I sew all my own costumes?"

Scotty nodded, her dark brown eyes flitting from me to the ice then back to me.

"When I was around your age, maybe a little older, I signed up for home economics as an elective because I was desperate to get my hands on those sewing machines. The one I had at home was old and hidden in the basement because…well, just because, for now." Now was not the time to get into how much Clay disliked anything gay. Well, aside from the money a gay man made. He liked that damn well. "Anydoodles, I was the only boy to sign up for home economics, or 'domestic science' as they call it now. All the other boys flocked to wood shop."

"Did you get picked on for being in the girls' class?" Scotty asked.

"Unmercifully. And the names I was called. They were terrible."

"Brian Rothcote called me a freak and kicked me in the boy parts."

"Oh, baby, I am *so* sorry."

"He said I had balls and not a pussy so I'd better start acting like a boy."

"Dear heavens! How old is this troglodyte?"

Scotty looked at me. "He's eleven."

"Where does a child that young learn such nasty words?" I was stunned, sick with sadness, and more than a little pissed off. "I hope he got into trouble."

"Internet," Scotty sighed. "He got suspended. I don't want to go back to school. Mom said I could have today off but I have to go back tomorrow. Brian will be back on Friday." She pushed her hood back just a bit and looked right into my soul. "Should I wear pants instead of a skirt from now on? What did you do when the boys beat you up for sewing?"

"I added more darn sequins to my shirt," I told her,

and that was the truth. "That shirt was so sparkly the teacher needed sunglasses to grade it. Which she did. An A+, thank *you* very much."

I polished my painted nails on my bright green vest. Scotty giggled just a bit.

"Baby girl, do not let fear dull your vibrancy. There are always going to be people who are jealous of how fabulous you are. And they'll say mean things, and kick you. They may even hit you. But you keep wearing skirts and boots and backpacks with those adorable dogs on them, because it's who you are." I tapped her button nose.

She leaped up and threw her arms around my neck, hugging me so hard I had trouble pulling in a breath. I held her close. She smelled like vanilla.

"I love you, Trent. You're so brave."

Brave? Not hardly. My mind pulled up an image of Dieter. Now that was bravery. And courage. And passionate kisses and gruff snorts of laughter. How had I fallen so deeply so fast? And what was I to do about it?

Her mother's eyes caught mine. She was crying into her mittens. And now I was crying too. *Wonderful. There goes my liner.* I pulled away from the hug just a bit.

"So let's get to work on your axel jumps. Did you bring that precious red outfit with the ruby skirt?"

She nodded, then ran off to the girl's locker room. Mrs. Denning pressed two fingers to her lips, blew me a kiss, then climbed up into the seats to watch.

Okay, yes, now I was happy I'd taken that check from the hockey boys. This was a good place, and the children needed this rink and me. I'd have to dash them a note of thanks. And maybe ask where I could find a certain grinder who was going under the knife.

I WAS at the hospital when Dieter woke up the following morning. Sitting there in that stuffy hospital room, a bag of chocolate kisses on my lap from my quick stop in Hershey. Yes, I'd eaten a candy bar on the way. Two hours behind the wheel of a rental car had made me anxious. Don't judge me.

His first reaction was slow, as if he were still battling the torpidity of the remnants of anesthesia. But then his eyes cleared. And I mean they were clear. Not blown out as if he were pumped full of narcotics.

"Trent." His voice was thick with sleep and pain, but soft. I smiled at Dieter.

"Morning."

He tried to sit up. I rushed to my feet to help him. He seemed to enjoy my flittering around like a nurse, stuffing pillows behind him.

"Do you want the nurse?"

"No, I'm happy to see you here instead of him. He's got this weird nose. It freaks me out."

"Okay." I sat back down, then placed the bag of candy beside him. "Those are for you because I can't give you real kisses."

"Why not?" He pawed at the bag resting by his hip, then lifted it to inspect it.

"Because you're just out of the operating room and…"

"That was yesterday."

"Oh, well, still, you're freshly operated upon." I reached out to flatten the wrinkles out of the crisp white sheet.

"They didn't cut my lips."

My gaze darted from the bedding to that luscious mouth of his. "No, but we need time not kissing so we can figure out where we're going in life."

"I'm going home and then into rehab. You look nice

today. Casual. No color in your hair, but with color on your lips and your eyes lined. Please don't stop doing that. I love you in makeup." He sat holding his candy, staring at me as if I were sweeter than the chocolate in his hands. It made me feel warm and special to be looked at like that.

"I was going for laid-back friend visit," I quipped, motioning to my smartly fitted jeans and the gray *#Filipino* T-shirt I'd pulled on. In truth, I'd just grabbed clothes after texting Layton to find out which hospital Dieter was in.

"So, we're just friends?" He looked a little pale in the morning sun filling the room. The medicinal smell was unpleasant. Maybe I should have brought flowers instead of candy.

"I think we're past friends."

"Me too." He shuffled a bit, grimaced, then ripped the bag of candy open. Little foil-wrapped droplets of chocolate flew over him and the bed, a few landing on the floor. "Grab a kiss."

I did, and slowly unwrapped it. Then I held it on my tongue until it melted. Dieter watched me intently as he chewed. We soon had a pile of tiny balls of foil and little paper ribbons mounded up on his bed.

"I'm so glad you're doing this," I finally said. "It takes courage to face your fears and get straight."

"They're giving me a chance, the Railers." He tossed me another kiss. I wished I could taste his mouth. I'd bet the combination of chocolate and Dieter would curl my little toes. "I don't want to fuck up this opportunity. Hockey is the biggest love of my life."

"I understand that. The lure of the ice, the feel of it under your skates, the drive to be the best you can be." I was terribly thirsty. I poured myself a glass of dusty water from the pitcher on the rolling stand beside his bed. Someone wearing squeaky shoes hurried past his door.

"It's hard to leave that behind, to turn away from competition."

"You did," he pointed out. His hair needed combing. My fingers would be perfect for the job. I took a sip of water instead.

"Due to mental duress. I'm back to coaching the kids at the rink." I refilled the plastic cup and passed it to him. He emptied it quickly, then asked for another.

"I bet you're a great coach."

"Thanks. It's fulfilling." I took the empty cup and rolled it between my hands. "I've missed you. I've worried about you. They're not giving you anything addictive in that, are they?" I jerked my head at the IV drip attached to his right arm.

"Nah, dammit."

"Dieter—"

"I was kidding. I'm okay, I guess. I missed you too. I miss the taste of that gloss and the way you feel tight up against me."

"We're quite the twitterpated pair, aren't we?"

"Guess so." He sighed.

"Can I come see you in rehab? It's only about two hours from Philly. I'll be happy to make the drive on the days the kids or the rink don't need me."

"What about the show? Don't they need you?"

"The Railers have gone home now, and I lost the cameras just outside Lancaster, so maybe I'll be fired. Fingers crossed," I whispered, then giggled impishly.

Dieter snickered, then offered me more candy.

I shook my head. "A moment on the lips…"

"Your ass is fine. I bet those jeans really make it look nice." His green-gold eyes were smoldering as he spoke. I stood up and gave him a slow spin. "Oh, hell yeah, they look damn good. When you come see me in rehab, wear them and another T-shirt."

"When can I come? Next week I have Wednesday free."

"I'll have to let you know. The first couple of weeks is no visitors. We're supposed to be bonding with the staff and our fellow dopers." He swallowed and sighed dismally. "I can't believe I have to do this again."

"I'll text you every day. Maybe send you random pictures of my ass in whatever pants I'm wearing, or a dick pic if you're exceptionally good."

That made him smile widely. My god, what that smile did to me. It made me silly and sad and scared and simpering.

"Dieter, I'm worried about me. What makes me seek out men with dependency issues? I think it's because I grew up with Clay. They say that what you grow up with you tend to become. Like children who grow up witnessing domestic violence seem to repeat that behavior as adults. Not all, of course, but many. Maybe I pick men with addictions because I grew up with a gambler..."

I paused when I realized what had just fallen out of my mouth. I hadn't vocalized it before. It felt good to have it out free. Was Dieter upset? Shit, how could he not be? Ugh. I'm such a loose-lipped Nellie.

"Yeah, maybe." He looked like his mind had gone on a stroll. "You ever think about talking to someone? I want to touch you. May I?"

"Please." I scooted closer and placed my hand into his. His fingers closed over mine. We both sighed softly. Yes, his skin next to mine did make the dawn a lot brighter. "Dieter, what I said about addicts – well, you know that's not the only reason I'm attracted to you. I'm just talking because I don't know what else to do with myself."

"If you figure out why you like fucked-in-the-head guys…will you break up with me?"

"Are we a couple?" My heart sped up at the mere thought of us together.

"In my heart, I think we are."

His fear choked me. Combined with mine, it was enough to bury a man. "I feel the same in my heart. And no, I will not break up with you. You're stuck with me, Lehmann – lip gloss, eyeliner, sequins and all."

He lifted my knuckles to his dry-looking lips. The kiss he pressed to them made me weepy and wanton. I was falling in love with him. Could two messes like him and me really make a relationship work? No, we couldn't. Not as we were now. But maybe with some help and some counseling…well, maybe we *could*. We'd have to love and know ourselves better first. I was willing to do that, to struggle to get centered and happy with Trent so that I could be whole and ecstatic with Dieter.

"I'm looking forward to being stuck with you, Hanson."

I stood up and stole a kiss. Not a chocolate one, either.

TWELVE

Dieter

A lyssa Albright was crying. She did a lot of that, but I didn't blame her. In these sessions where we sat in a circle in the bright room and talked about the shit in our heads, at times all I wanted to do was sit and cry.

"And I still didn't lose that extra ten pounds," she was saying between sobs, "even though I hadn't eaten for a week, and my partner refused to work on the lifts because he said I was a heifer, and shit..." She buried her face in her hands.

She was a figure skater, oddly enough. She wasn't at Trent's level, more Disney on Ice, but she and I had the ice in common, and over the last two weeks we'd gravitated toward each other. She couldn't weigh more than a hundred pounds, and that was being generous. She suffered from an eating disorder, an addiction to meds; she was a broken kid who at twenty-five looked about sixteen.

"You're tiny," I blurted out, then sat back in my chair. We were encouraged to discuss and comment, but not when someone was still telling a story. Had she finished? I wasn't sure.

"Not tiny enough," she said, so sadly it made my heart hurt.

"My friend is a figure skater," I said, and she looked at me.

I was beginning to reveal bits and pieces in this session. Family stuff, medical information. The guys in this room all knew I was a hockey player. I wasn't anything special in here, not that I wanted to be, but whatever, I was sitting with a figure skater, two footballers, one freaky-tall basketball dude, a surgeon, and a librarian.

Although I was sure that the librarian was a cover, because Ethel looked like she was on constant state of alert and kept making this motion like she was reaching for a gun. I was thinking CIA or special ops or some kind of freaky Jason Bourne shit. And who the hell used Ethel as a cover name? Not that I was expecting her name to be Pussy Galore, but still…

"He is?" Alyssa asked, and side-eyed me.

"Yeah, and he would be able to pick you up, because he's strong and focused and works with his partners." I didn't know that last part, but Trent was the kind of man who would do his best by anyone he worked with, I was sure of it. "Anyway, you come to my rink, and I have an entire team who could pick you up and carry you around like you were made of air. The guy who told you that, he'd clearly missed his workouts."

She smiled at me; that broken, crooked, tear-filled smile. She probably didn't believe me, so I did something really stupid. I blame the lack of exercise other than in the small gym on-site, I blame not being out on the ice, but in my head I just wanted to do something for someone else.

I stood up and offered a hand, and she took it and stood with me.

"What?" she asked, peering up at me from her five foot five.

In a smooth move, I scooped her up in my arms. I was right; there was nothing to her. She squealed and laughed, but at least she wasn't crying. "Alyssa, any professional skater whose job it is to lift you should find it easier than lifting a pillow. It's not your fault he dropped you – that was all on him."

She got a stupid look on her face, then grinned. "Lift me higher."

So I did.

And then I took the challenge of lifting basketball dude, Dave, who was all arms and legs.

I drew the line at lifting the football guys – I mean, they were seriously built and both there for help with steroid abuse. And I still had a bum knee, or at least a healing, somewhat sore knee.

Ethel raised a single eyebrow, and I knew she was telegraphing that if I picked her up she would kill me with a single blow.

When I sat down again, though, the mood of the room had lightened, and the tears that came after, from Dave and some from myself, were cathartic.

Back in my room, I had two phone calls to make. The first one I was dreading, the second I wanted much more. No one would actually know if I didn't make that first call. No one but me.

Mom answered on the fourth ring like she always did, always checking the caller ID and then stumbling over which button to press to answer the call. I'd seen her do it so many times, and the thought of her staring at the phone and fumbling with it made me smile.

"Hey, Mom."

"Sorry, who are you? Do we know anyone called Dieter?"

"Ha ha," I said. "I know it's been a while."

"A week is a while. A month is grounds for us putting you up for adoption. Although no one would want you now you've gone past the cute puppy stage."

She was teasing me, and I could hear the smile in her voice. I loved my parents, twenty-seven years married and still in love even now. They'd worked hard for me, got up for every practice, watched all my games; they were the kind of self-sacrificing hockey parents that every kid who wanted to strap on skates should have.

Of course, my mom had been a figure skater – not professionally, but she'd once got very close to selection for the Olympic team. But she'd fallen with me, and to this day she said she'd take me over a medal.

That was what made my heart hurt so bad.

I'd let her down, my dad as well, and I'd kept it all a secret. Only this was a Bad Thing, according to my therapy group. I needed to be honest and open and look for the best in my life, which was my parents, hockey, and now Trent. I didn't have siblings, I knew my parents had tried after me, but it just hadn't happened. I was their hope for everything.

"Do you have ten minutes?" I asked, to pull myself back to the here and now. Part of me hoped she would say she had to be somewhere.

"Always," she said. "I'll just grab a coffee and sit in the kitchen."

I heard her moving around, imagined the kitchen with its worn counters and the big range. It sounds idyllic, and believe me, it was. My mom was a real mom, just like in all the advertisements you see on the TV, or in an old episode of *The Waltons*. She ran the family, she and my dad never argued, and she did it with love.

"Okay," she said. "Shoot. Is this about the knee? Are they sending you back to the Rush? I'm sorry, hun, but you can work your way back, and you know they want you."

"No, Mom, the knee is good, rehab is good, and I'm hoping to get back on the ice with the Railers after the start of the season."

"We want tickets, sweetie."

"Always," I said, repeating her earlier word. Every game I ever played there were tickets for Pauline and Gustav Lehmann, and most of the time they managed at least ten or so games. "That wasn't why I was phoning. I'm not at home at the moment. I'm at the hospital; well kind of."

"But you said your knee... Dieter?" She sounded suddenly fearful, and I couldn't leave things at that point too long.

"When I first hurt my knee, I had strong meds, and I became addicted to them. I kicked it, but it grabbed me back. I'm in rehab, Mom."

Silence for a second longer than I'd hoped, and I imagined her heart breaking.

"I'm glad you got some help," she said finally.

"Mom, I'm sorry—"

"But most of all, I'm so proud of you for getting help, and for telling me."

I teared up. Right there and then, I could have bawled like a fricking baby. Imagine that on reality TV – *hockey player loses his shit on phone to his mom*.

"Mom..."

"I know, Dieter. I know, sweetheart. I'm here, talk to me."

And the dam wall broke.

When I'd cried all the tears and heard everything my mom had to say, she promised to talk to dad. She told me he would be fine, and I knew she was right. He was the other half of her, and they thought so much the same.

I just worried that being a man, my dad would be more difficult to talk to. When my cell rang within two minutes of my mom getting off the phone, I knew I wouldn't have long to wait. We didn't cry, but we did the phone version of manly back-slapping, and he reassured me that he was in my corner, then called me an idiot for not telling them sooner.

We talked about how it upset Mom; that was our way of admitting how we felt about it affecting us as father and son.

"I love you, Dieter, always remember that."

"I love you too, Dad."

I texted Trent, told him about Alyssa, and didn't think about how I wasn't ready to tell Mom and Dad about Trent as well as my addiction.

I would call them tomorrow about him. Make them see the two things weren't related in any way.

I left a voicemail because he didn't answer, but he was out there living a life, he wasn't there by the phone waiting to text me back at the drop of a hat. He was visiting today; the first one. Not supervised or any of that shit, but he'd have to sign in, and be checked, and he wasn't allowed to bring in food or drink. I think he was disappointed; he'd said he wanted to bring in his grandma's food as a picnic.

So I'd set up something myself. I'd organized with the kitchen, had a small container of food prepared – nothing special, but lots of protein, which I still had access to. No sense in going into rehab and coming out unable to get back to skating. I took my exercise and my eating very seriously. Anyway, I didn't eat half as much as the football guys, who could clear a table in ten seconds flat.

I counted down the time; he was due to be there at four p.m., and I had a shower, wore my best jeans and a clean T-shirt, and waited just outside reception.

He was there at three fifty-seven, signing in, filling in forms, and he couldn't see me from where I was, but I could certainly see him.

And he looked good.

His hair was a vibrant blue again, but he'd had it cut; it was shorter at the back. I couldn't see clearly what kind of makeup he wore, but I hoped to hell he'd gone the whole way. He certainly hadn't skimped on what he was wearing; electric blue pants, a silver-and-sapphire shirt, and plenty of splashy bangles on his wrists. There was no such thing as incognito for Trent Hanson.

I saw the receptionist hand him his security pass, and waited by the door as she gestured toward it with instructions of where he should go. And then he was there.

And I didn't touch him. The door closed behind him, the locks clicking, and he was there.

"Trent," I said, and pushed my hands into my jeans pockets, because I didn't know what to do with them.

"Hey," he said, and put a hand on his hip. He looked a little unsure, as if he wasn't entirely convinced I wanted him to be there. What was I doing? Why wasn't I putting myself out there, exposing myself to the man I wanted?

I'm brave. I can do this.

I stepped forward until there wasn't much space between us and he had to look up at me. I cradled his beautiful face in my hands and just closed my eyes.

The kiss was soft and right and it was everything I needed right there.

But what about Trent? He didn't kiss me back with his

usual enthusiasm, or hold me, or make a single sound. I stopped the kiss and backed away, and he looked at me with his head tilted a little.

"Is it okay to kiss?" he asked uncertainly. I didn't think he meant it in an I'm-gay-what-will-people-say kind of way, I think he meant something about how it would upset my recovery.

I held out a hand, which he took, and led him down the main corridor and through the door to the extensive grounds.

"How's the knee?" he said.

I was limping, the leg was braced, but I'd stopped using the crutches. "I'm doing good," I said as we walked on the grass and climbed the hill up to the stand of trees that was my thinking spot.

He didn't say anything else.

"When I first got here, they said I needed to find a place here where I could sit and think," I explained, and stopped under the biggest of the red maples. I momentarily released my hold on his hand, slipped off my backpack of hoarded goodies, and awkwardly clambered down to sit cross-legged. He copied me, and we were sitting close to each other. "Kissing is good," I said, answering his question.

At first the kisses were soft, and he was enthusiastic and obviously into it as much as me, and then abruptly it turned from affection to lust, and he climbed me like a freaking monkey, sprawling over me and levering me flat on the ground, always staying away from my knee. I straightened my legs a little to get comfy, and he sat back – sitting right over my hard cock, which was definitely into his visit – and stared down at me.

"Tell me everything," he ordered.

Wait. What? Had he missed the part where he was

sitting on my cock and wiggling? So I summarized, in the hope I might get some friction going.

"Two-week report, all good, managing expectations, group chats, lifted a figure skater today, usual stuff, hope to get out to the gym next week to work on fitness, knee is healing fine, and I have PT."

"I'm really proud of you," he said softly, then took each of my hands in his and leaned down, pressing my hands into the grass. I'd never felt so vulnerable as with the naked pride in Trent's eyes. All I'd done was what I should have done two years ago when I first got hurt. It wasn't heroic to face my own decisions. It wasn't something that meant people should be proud of me.

It was up to me to be proud of myself. To know myself. Wasn't that the message they were selling me?

I was certainly buying into it and beginning to feel like I had other options.

"In the first meeting I told myself I hadn't actually meant to take the meds this time," I said, his lips only just a little away from mine. I could lean up, he could move a little, we could be kissing, but this was one thing I wanted him to know. "I was lying. I took them because they made things right in my head. I was in pain, and I couldn't relax. They helped with the pain, then more made it easier to relax."

"Okay." He kissed me then, just a simple kiss to the end of my nose.

"And also, there's this whole mentality of playing through the pain, and I wanted so badly to get to the NHL that I was willing to take a shortcut around the pain I was feeling."

"Okay," he murmured, and kissed an eyelid. It felt like I was getting a kiss for everything I revealed about myself. A game. I liked games.

"I feel like a fraud, like one day the Railers will wake up and tell me they never meant to offer me a contract."

That earned me a kiss to the other eyelid and a soft buzz of his skin on my cheek. I could smell him, the clean scent of the air around us, and I focused on every small part of him, his weight pinning me to the ground, his determined gaze.

"I want to play hockey with the Railers. I want to do that so bad; I worry that if I can't reach that final dream then I won't be me anymore."

This time he kissed my lips gently.

"But most of all, I have to stop the pills for me."

The kisses deepened, and we just lay there, under the tree, and kissed for the longest time.

"So, my stepdad," Trent said.

"Yeah? What about him?"

"He's been asking to see me. Asking my mom to tell me he wants me to visit him. That he has things to say to me."

"How do you feel about that?"

His nose crinkled. "Not enough time in this visit to cover it all."

Trent went really quiet then, so I told him funny stories, and he was soon laughing, particularly when I ended up with the lifting story. He reared back a little.

"I looked Alyssa up," he said. "Watched her on YouTube; she's got style." He wriggled against me and my cock perked up again. "I could lift her easy, and look at me."

"I *am* looking at you." Possibly the most redundant thing I'd ever said. "You're gorgeous."

He wrinkled his nose. He was freaking adorable at that moment, and I stole another kiss as best I could without using my hands to drag him down.

He rolled up and off me, lying on his back at my side.

"I missed you," he said, then half rolled back so he was leaning on me. I wanted him back on top of me. Now. "I'm hungry, what did you get?"

He sat up and pulled at the bag behind me, opening it up and pulling items out one by one. I wanted his kisses, not to eat, but I realized he had a point when my stomach growled. In the shade we ate PB & Js, chips, and drank water, and through it all he was telling me about his kids, and the rink, and how this kid called Scotty needed someone to talk to, and how he felt good that he could help.

"So when are they letting you… I mean…saying you can leave."

"I could leave now," I said with a smile as he tripped over his words. "I'm not, though. I have a trainer working with me from next week, and there'll be visits to this gym nearby. What happens now is completely in my hands."

"What about the team? Have you heard anything from them?"

That was actually one of the most surprising things. I'd expected something from Connor; he was the kind of captain who had a team mate's back. I'd guessed I'd hear from Toly as my rep, and his texts were written half in Russian, which meant I had to translate them. That was to give me something to do, according to his most recent message.

But it was the others. Ten sent me stupid jokes. Stan sent me texts that he'd clearly written through Google translate, because they made me laugh as much as Ten's jokes. Arvy sent me a really well-considered and thoughtful "thinking of you, man" text. I could even imagine the bro-hug that would go with it. Then there was Layton's message. That was a little more serious, and even though he worded it carefully, he wanted to give me a heads-up that Marianna had contacted him directly wanting to discuss the situation in light of my new contract. He said she'd visited the rink, for fuck's sake, but that he'd shut it down.

I needed to get back out there, deal with her, give Arvy a bro-hug, find some jokes in English and Russian for Ten and Stan.

Mostly I needed to go back out and have myself a rebuilding month or two.

"I've heard from a lot of them," I finally answered. "But none of the messages mean as much as the ones I get from you."

Silence. He didn't look away, but he didn't gush enthusiastically about our communication. If anything, he went a little quiet and thoughtful.

"I need to make a move," Trent announced to break the silence. He hopped to his feet, brushed off crumbs and held out a hand. "C'mon, big guy."

"Did I say something wrong?" I asked, worried I'd fucked up big time.

Trent helped me to stand and brushed me down as well, like I had an entire loaf of crumbs on me, then he stopped and sighed.

"I want to get naked with you," he admitted, and where there had been worry before, now I felt all kinds of happy. "But we can't, so you shouldn't say stuff like that which gets me all worked up."

We held hands walking down the hill. Me hobbling now, him trying to walk at my pace, his steps bouncing. Then he shook off my hand and jumped down the final part, helping me down, which I have to admit I really needed. Then he darted away, and I realized he was headed right for Alyssa, who looked so startled she nearly fell off her chair. He said something to her, and then before

I could reach them, he had her up in his arms, and with a complicated roll she was on his shoulder and they were in some kind of complex-looking lift.

Right there in the garden.

She was laughing. He was grinning.

Oh god. I have this so bad, this new addiction. Trent.

I am so in love.

THIRTEEN

Trent

L ate summer crept past, or so it seemed. Seeing Dieter once a week, if I had time, was simply not enough. I needed more. I *wanted* more. More touching and talking, more intimacy. Grinding against each other under that red maple wasn't cutting it anymore. Texting was okay, but lacking in many ways. Video calls helped. I could see his sparkling green eyes and that incredible jaw of his all covered with scruff, but I couldn't touch those whiskers or kiss the corners of those jade eyes. Yet I knew he was where he needed to be. Still, my body ached for his touch. I was a greedy goose. Fall was in the air now; it tickled the senses on cool mornings, then disappeared as the seasons battled for control. Today was one of those ungodly humid and hot early September days in the city. Clothing stuck to skin, hair flopped and makeup ran.

Trent was not a happy camper. And things looked to be getting much worse.

My mother hurried out of her little row house, dressed to the nines, a smile brightening her face. That smile fell when she saw the van parked behind her car. Inside that white van sat a camera crew, sound men and makeup. All waiting anxiously for us to get into the old beater Chevy Impala mom owned and drive to Mercer County. To see Clay.

"Why are those cameras here?" Mom pushed out through gritted teeth.

I dabbed at my sweaty brow with a hankie that matched my mauve pants. I was feeling rather Prince today. You know, sexy and sassy and proud of it? I'd colored my hair deep purple the night before, and dressed in shades of purple and hot pink right down to the raspberry beret seated on my plum-colored hair and my sparkly raspberry truffle boots. This kind of display – all the frippery and feminine colors – would probably make my stepfather's head explode. He and I had to have this meeting. It would only be the once, but I wanted him to see me as I was. He would deal with colorful Trent or he could go back to his cell.

"They're here because I have a contract."

She planted her feet and glowered at the van and then at me.

"Supposedly this visit to prison will make for 'gripping, powerful and dramatic reality television', according to the producer."

"I hate that you're broadcasting such private things to millions of people."

"I hate that Clay stole all my money and forced me into broadcasting private things to millions of people just to keep your house and my rink out of the bank's hands."

Her anger seemed to fade away. Wished this heat would. I was so edgy and irritable when I was uncomfortable.

"I'm sorry for that," she said for the one billionth time.

"Mom, stop apologizing for him. His actions are his

own. We learned that in family counseling last week, remember?"

"Yes, yes, I remember. I just feel like…"

"I know." I gave her a tremulous smile and waved a limp handkerchief at her car. "Can we get going? I'm melting."

"Okay, yes." She shot the crew a worried look, but hustled around her car and got behind the wheel.

The windows had been up to discourage anyone stealing her Tony Orlando & Dawn cassette tapes. As if any thief would burgle cassette tapes of Tony Orlando & Dawn – nothing personal, Tony. It was like sitting down inside one of Beelzebub's blast furnaces. She rolled down her window, and a soothing hot blast of Philadelphia air rolled into the car.

"Much better," I said. Mom picked up the snide and turned the air-conditioning on. "Thank you. I'll pay for the gas the cold air sucks up."

We pulled out into traffic and rode along in silence for a bit. "He's excited that you're coming," Mom finally said.

"Ugh."

I began picking at the nail polish on my thumb. Mom sighed. I stopped picking and replied with words, just like our therapist had instructed us. Well, me. She had instructed *me* to use words instead of sounds, grunts, or rude hand gestures when my stepfather was mentioned. "I've really got nothing to say to him."

"He has things to say to you. He loves you."

"Pfft." I squeezed my eyes shut, then corrected myself. "I mean I highly doubt that. He's never loved me. He tolerated me for you. He might love you, but I was always the little queer kid who embarrassed him at the track."

"You know, for a man who's dating someone who's

battled with addiction, you're pretty damn judgmental about another person with the same problem."

I stared out the window on my right, watching the cityscape fade away. That one hurt. It hurt because it was true. I'd only told my mother about Dieter last week. She'd asked because I'd used his name a time or two, but I'd refused to share that with her. Doctor Penny, our new counselor, had encouraged me to be frank and honest. So I'd told mom about my new boyfriend. She'd been happy yet worried, which I got. She'd gone through the whole Jonah thing. But this was different. Dieter was doing well and would stay that way.

Please god, let him stay straight. My heart couldn't take that again.

"I'm not in a good place with Clay yet, Mom," I confessed about ten minutes after the original flurry of angry.

"I know, babes. I know." She patted my thigh, then hit the blinkers.

My gaze roamed over the massive minimum-security facility. I had never been inside a place that was surrounded by electric fencing topped with barbed wire.

"Don't be freaked out when they search you."

"No, I won't be. They do that up at Dieter's rehab center," I murmured as we climbed out and met the TV crew.

I wondered what kind of special permission the station had had to procure to allow this to happen. My stomach was a knotted-up mess. I hadn't eaten since yesterday afternoon. How I wished Dieter were there to hang on to.

Our cars and our bodies were searched before we even took a step. After that bit of fun, I offered my hand to my mother. She took it, and we walked to the entrance. The camera crew followed. At the gate, I spun to face them.

"You're not coming in," I announced. They all sighed. Guessed they were used to Trent throwing himself. Good. This would come as no surprise, then.

"Trent," the producer cajoled, "we've been over this a hundred times. You signed a contract stating that you'd give us one hundred hours of film. If you keep balking at every little thing that twists your titties, we're going to have to call the powers that be and tell them you're not living up to your contractual obligations."

"Call them. I don't care. My mother is upset by your presence. This is a personal family matter, and you are not welcome."

"Trent, for Christ's sake, reality television is all *about* personal family matters. That's what makes the genre so fucking appealing." He was giving it his best, but I wasn't budging. I'd seen the distaste on Mom's face, felt her unease now. "People at home want to know that you celebrities live lives that are more fucked up than theirs."

"Well, tough shit for the viewing public."

I turned away from the film crew, tightened my grip on my mother's hand, and led her into the prison. I'd probably end up being sued before this was all said and done. So be it.

"Thank you, baby," Mom whispered.

I squeezed her fingers, and we entered the depths of the corrections facility.

All the permission forms were in order. We'd all adhered to the dress code, aside from the bangles on my wrists. Those had to be left with a guard. We were patted down yet again once inside, then asked to go through a metal detector. I could hear the inmates. I was sick with nerves. We were escorted to a private room. Prisoners walked past. Catcalls and lewd proposals drifted over us.

Thankfully, the guards assigned to this dog-and-pony show kept the men in orange moving along.

Once inside the private visitation area that had been set aside for the show, Mom sat down at the table.

The door opened and Clay entered, followed by a guard the size of Mount Rushmore. My empty stomach cramped. Clay looked the same only older. So much older. And haggard. His dark hair was neatly trimmed, but his swarthy complexion was sallow. His gaze went around the room as he was led to his seat. I was glad to see no handcuffs were in place.

"I'm Corrections Officer Kent, and I'll be right in that corner," Mount Rushmore informed us, then went to said corner to stand and be silently intimidating. Was that how things always went, or was he there because of the TV show that was supposed to happen?

Mom sat down across from Clay. I stood in the opposite corner from CO Kent, chewing my thumbnail, feeling angry and queasy all at once. Mom and Clay joined hands and let them lie on the table.

"Good to see you, Donna. You look so pretty," Clay said. The timbre of his voice after so long made me twitchy. Then his gaze left my mother and settled on me. "Good to see you as well, Trent. You're so...colorful today."

"You mean gay. I'm so gay today. That *is* what you meant, right, Inmate Gallo?" My hand fell to my side.

Clay's dark eyes flared. Then he nodded. "I deserve that dislike from you. I did you wrong, son."

The tight rubber band keeping me together snapped. "No. Oh, no! You do *not* call me son!" I yelled and pointed a finger at his long face. "I am *not* your son. You made that clear years ago. Remember all those times you called me a little fag for liking figure skating and sewing?"

He dropped his head in shame, but not before I could see that his eyes were filled with remorse. "That was wrong of me."

"No shit. So was stealing all my money! I was this fucking close to a breakdown." He glanced at me. I showed him a millimeter of space between my thumb and forefinger. "I've had to pimp myself out to fucking reality shows and hockey teams to keep your wife from living on the streets." My hands were flying around, the gesticulations wild and heated. "I fucking *hate* you. I hate what you did to us, and I hate how you think you can just walk back into our lives and everyone will accept you because you're an addict."

"He's not thinking that, Trent. Not at all," Mom interjected, her eyes pleading. "Doesn't he deserve a second chance like your Dieter?"

"Do not *ever* bring up my boyfriend in defense of this asshole," I barked at my mother. "He's off working harder than he has *ever* worked before trying to get straight and make amends to me and his team! This piece of shit is—"

"Trying to do the same thing, Trent," Clay chanced to say.

His words felt like a sledgehammer to the midsection. I bent over, eyes closed, working on pulling in oxygen. Someone touched my back. I whirled away from the touch and went back to my corner, silent tears making a mess of my eyeliner and mascara.

"I'm trying to make things right even though I know I can never really do that. Apologizing to you for the years gambling had me in its grip is tough, but part of my recovery. I've already admitted that I was powerless over gambling. I've committed myself to turning my life around, and making amends to the people I harmed is part of the program."

"I can't hear your apology right now. I need to hate you more," I gasped, and battled with hyperventilating.

"That's okay, I understand," Clay softly replied. My mother started weeping quietly. "I'm going to keep trying to make things right with you and your mother."

I nodded in understanding, then bolted from the room, hand over my mouth. I found a trash can before I could locate a bathroom, so I dry-heaved over that. Thank goodness, the bag had recently been replaced. When the heaves stopped, I swiped a hand over my lips, smearing the gloss terribly, I was sure. I stood up. My mother was walking toward me, looking so pretty in a yellow summer dress with her jet-black hair pulled back from her face.

"I'm such a hypocrite," I coughed just as her arms went around my waist.

"No, babes, you're not. It's harder to forgive than it is to hate." She pressed a kiss to my damp cheek. "You'll get there. You're a good man, kind and giving, and so loving."

"Can we go? I have to go…and think about this mess. My happy level is monstrously low."

"Let's go home. Your grandmother is making a special meal for us."

We left the prison and Clay behind. The crew hustled out to catch up with us. I watched the facility growing smaller and smaller in the side mirror while my ability to breath slowly returned. Mom said nothing the whole way home, just smiled on occasion. I chewed on the inside of my mouth, sight blurred, mind spinning madly, until we pulled up outside the old brick house on 16th Avenue and I saw Dieter waiting by the curb.

I threw the door open before we were even parked properly. The van carrying the crew parked behind us in the middle of the street. I ran at Dieter, tears flowing again, and launched myself at him. He caught me with ease, his strong hands cupping my ass. I wrapped my arms and legs around him and captured his mouth with mine. The taste of him healed me. And then reality hit me. Well, the knowledge of a reality *show* hit me.

"Oh hell," I whispered.

"Surprised to see me?" he joked when we came up for air.

"Forgive me. I just outed you to the world. I'll tell them to stop filming."

"No, it's good. Let the world know about us. Hiding things is what got me into this mess. I'm not hiding anything ever again."

I peppered his face with kisses, the cameras circling us slowly. I dove back in for another hot kiss, this one lasting so long I felt woozy.

"I thought you were staying in rehab for another week," I panted a moment later.

"Couldn't stay away from you any longer." His smile was sinful and soft. I kissed him again and again and yet again.

"Trent, let's go inside. Grandma is setting up *kamayan*."

Dieter released me, and my feet settled to the sidewalk. I ran a finger along Dieter's jaw, then turned to look at my mother.

"This is Dieter."

"Yes, I assumed." She leaned in to kiss his scruffy cheek, then led us inside her house, pointedly leaving the TV show on the curb.

"Um, what's *kamayan*?" Dieter asked as we headed directly to the kitchen.

I caressed his back and hip. I just couldn't get enough tactile contact.

"It's big, happy meal," *Lola* said, waving her hands toward the food resting on the table. A long line of rice rested on banana leaves, with piles of roasted vegetables and glazed meats like pork and chicken. My stomach roared. "You still play for Harrisburg?" She crossed her arms over her Dave Schultz jersey.

"Yes, ma'am," Dieter replied. I wiggled into his side.

"Still sucky team, but welcome to house for making my grandson smile so big. Wash hands. Go now then sit down."

I nudged him toward the sink. "Better wash up before she calls you something worse."

"Like being told my team sucks isn't bad enough?"

"Philly fans are rough." I laughed and felt the weight of life leaving me. Dieter chuckled and stole a fast kiss.

Then we ate. Seated at the table, we stuffed ourselves using only our fingers, as is custom for *kamayan* feasts. I was so full I thought I might faint, but that was also part of the custom.

Dieter and I helped to clean up, then we went off to find couple time to talk. I knew that if we went back to my place, talking would be the last thing happening. Also, I wanted to show him off to my city. The van was gone, which was a good thing.

"I cannot *wait* for the end of the week," I told him as we walked to my scooter. "Just six more days and they'll have enough footage for an eight-episode pilot season."

"What are you going to do if they pick it up?"

"Die inside." I unlocked the helmet and handed it to him. "Pray they find me too flashy. I'm tired of the limelight. I just want to coach my kids and spend time with my boyfriend."

"And who would that be?" He stood there so tall and handsome, yellow helmet in hand, giving me shade. I rather liked his teasing, but would never admit it.

"Some big doofus in a Railers T-shirt. Get on."

"That will never hold me." He shoved the helmet at me. I pushed it back. "Seriously, do you know how stupid that will look with me on the back?"

"Since when do we care what looks stupid to other people?"

And that, as they say, ended that.

We pulled up to Sister Cities Park around noon. Hundreds of people, adults and children, were enjoying the fountains as a way to cool down. I locked my helmet into place and took Dieter by the hand. The Cathedral of SS Peter and Paul looked down on us as we walked past a tiny concrete pond filled with small sailboats with red sails. After grabbing a drink at the café, we proceeded to find a spot in the shade beside a fountain that shot bursts of water into the air from alternating spots. Several kids in shorts splashed and played in the streams as traffic around Logan Square moved steadily.

"This is my favorite park in the city," I told him as we sipped iced tea.

"It's nice." He turned on the concrete bench to face me, holding his tea in his hands. "You look like someone punched you in the face."

Damn. I should have touched up my makeup before coming out. I wet a finger and tried scrubbing the area under my left eye. Dieter shook his head and tugged my finger gently downward. His hair was long, tickling the collar of his dusky blue T-shirt.

"It was a tough session with Clay," I explained, my fingers creeping up his arm to toy with those long strands.

"You want to talk about it?"

"Yes, but not now. Now, I want to talk about us."

Two teens on bikes rode by, racing through the fountain. I wasn't sure if bikes were allowed in the park, but I was too happy to call them out for it.

"Okay, what about us?"

I glanced up at the sun, the sky, and the fluffy white clouds moving over Philly. "Did you know that seeing you makes me feel like I was up there in the clouds?"

I peeked from the clouds to him. He'd tipped his head back to look. I leaned in and dropped a kiss to his Adam's apple, then sat back as straight as a ruler.

"That was nice. I like kissing in public." He seemed so relaxed. I wished we could stay there beside the playful fountain forever.

"That's good, because we made out in front of TV cameras. Will you get any flack for that?" I lifted my straw to my lips and sucked. The tea was sweet and lemony, perfect for a hot September day.

"I doubt it. I mean, we have Tennant and Jared. Anyone who comes after them will pale in comparison. They're paving the way for the rest of us. Plus it keeps Layton in work."

"Mmm, yes, they are. So brave. Okay, then, so we're now an official couple. And I live and work here," I waved a hand at the city, "and you live and work in the state capital. Can we make this work?"

"Do you love me?"

"More than YSL Couture eye pencils."

His brow furrowed. "That's like a lot of love then, right?"

"Simply tons." I slid closer and let my head drop to his broad shoulder. He slipped an arm around me. I was in heaven, even if my liner was smudged, and not in that fashionable way I sometimes wore it.

"Guess if we love each other that much we'll work it out. We'll get game schedules and arrange things around our home games. And we play Philly a lot, so I'll be in town at least six or seven times over the season."

"*Lola* will be torn about who to cheer for. I think she likes you."

"Oh, she won't be torn, trust me." He chortled and cinched me tighter to his side. "It's only two hours away. You might have to buy a car. Scooting to Harrisburg in January might be more than even you can handle."

"For you, I'll buy a car. It will have to be flashy, though."

"I'd be disappointed if it were anything else."

Now that was true love right there.

FOURTEEN

Dieter

Walking back into East River Arena, it felt like I'd been away for years. I imagined it would all be changed, but the only thing that was different was that the security guard stepped out of his office and shook my hand. Normally we just exchanged nods and smiles, but he seemed determined for me to know that he was pleased I was there.

"Good to see you back," he announced, and pumped my hand furiously. "The boys needed you last game."

The Railers had already played two of their pre-season games, with their last one tomorrow, and had been soundly beaten by the Bruins, who shouldn't have been able to show us up quite so much. A seven–three loss wasn't something we needed to worry about – this was the pre-season, a way of getting the skating back in our bones. Still. Seven–three was more of a loss than had been expected.

"I'm not sure they did," I answered. I wasn't a key player like Ten, around whom the team was getting stronger, I was the hard worker who did his bit. The security guard – Emmet, according to his badge – was clearly

149

placing too much value on my position as a third line winger.

"Our wing is lacking," he said without hesitation. "You're a worker, a playmaker – hurry up back on the team."

We shook hands again, and for a moment I had to fight this insane need to grab the man close and hug him hard. Instead I smiled back at him and pivoted to take the corridors down to the locker rooms. I had PT after this first skate back on the ice, and I knew that Colin Pike would be there; the offensive coach was the one tasked with working on my fitness. I'd probably set one blade on the ice and fall on my ass like a fucking moron.

I stripped my clothes and began to put on my uniform from the under-layers up, taking careful time to make sure my knee brace was secure. Light skating – that was what I'd been told to do today. The doc, Colin, my PT, they all said I was ready to get back on the ice, but there was no date for playing.

Thank god. I was shaky on this damn knee, but at least there was no pain.

A couple of the guys were in the locker room, but I didn't think anything of it. Stan was there, muttering under his breath in Russian, likely some kind of goalie incantation to the gods of the net, but he did look up and nod as I came in. Then there was Arvy, semi-naked as usual, earbuds in, humming some tune that sounded way off-key. He at least took his earbuds out and shook my hand.

"Good to have you back, Deets," he said, and pulled me in for a sideways bro-hug.

Ten ambled in, fully attired, waddling a little on his skates, a broad grin on his face, his lips suspiciously puffy, like he'd been kissed a lot recently. Which was borne out when Jared followed him in looking all kinds of disheveled.

"Deets!" Ten shouted, and grabbed me in a full-body hug. I hugged him back. I didn't know why any of these guys were there at this ungodly hour of the morning, but I couldn't deny how happy I was to see them.

With my practice jersey in place, I made my way to the ice. Colin, offensive coach extraordinaire, was already there, sitting on a bench, hunched over his phone. He looked up at me and nodded.

This was the man who would be working with me to keep me a Railer. This was the guy who held my career in his hands. If he turned around and said I was done, then that was it, I was done. He inclined his head toward the ice, and I knew what he was saying.

The ice is yours; see how it goes.

For the longest time I stood on the rubber, cricking my neck, testing the feel of the stick in my hands, inhaling the icy air and grinning like an idiot.

The first glide, the press of blade on ice, and it felt like I'd never been away. The gentle motion as I skated forward, not too much weight on my bum knee, was soothing and quiet. The cold of the air touched my skin, and it was familiar and right. I skated in lazy circles, the crossovers in the corners a little cautious at first. Each time I pushed harder, and I was up to a good speed and there was no ache yet.

Best of all, having kept up with the cardio meant I wasn't breathing hard, at least not yet.

I sensed the others on the ice, and for a moment I was disappointed that I had to share the space, and then I realized what they were doing and why they were there. Each of them was skating alongside me, even Stan, and they were slow to be at my pace.

My eyes stung, but I wasn't going to give in and cry like a fucking idiot on the ice.

They talked as we skated, hockey gossip, trade rumors, teams they liked for the cup, teams they wished they could beat, teams they guessed would beat them.

The conversation only grew tight when Ten mentioned something about his parents visiting and Stan went really quiet and nearly fell over, sliding into the boards in one goalie-kit mess. The first thing you do when a teammate falls on the ice is to chirp them, but something about his expression screamed for us all to back off.

So we did.

"His mama refuse to come from Russia," Toly confided as we held back.

The session was about me. Pike took me through some gentle exercises. I wasn't right, not fixed, and I was far from able to play in a game, but the cat-calling from the guys, and their tacit support, made me think I could be back there doing this and not make an idiot of myself.

When I came off the ice I was high on life, not on meds, and I couldn't wait to share it with someone.

In the locker room, I checked my phone. My parents had texted. My mom was all about the pride she had in me. Dad was all about pain levels and included all kinds of medical questions. I sent back a group text to them with enough of both subjects to keep them both happy.

And then there was Trent's text.

A simple heart emoji.

We'd talked the night before, about agents managing my social media accounts; I'd been put right in the middle of rumors about me and Trent, even though the program wasn't even out yet. A few grainy stills that I needed someone to manage. His agent said she'd take me on if I was interested. I needed to give her an answer.

"You want to come up for a chat?" Layton asked from the doorway.

My immediate answer? No, I really didn't, but there was a lot more to this complete shitfest that was my life than just the knee and being outed; there was Marianna and her blackmail.

I nodded, and after a shower I headed to his office. He had a much larger space now, and a window, and one thing I noticed was that he wasn't so nervous-looking when I closed the door behind me. I always felt too big around him, like I was one of the hockey giants who intimidated him.

"Have a seat," he said, and slid a coffee across the table. "So, I want to take this to the authorities."

"What?" I was horrified at the idea of this being taken outside the small circle of trust I had going on. "No, we have to deal with this ourselves."

Layton held up a hand to stop me, and I had to trust that he knew what he was doing. Even if my instincts were shouting at me to stop.

"I'd like to file an official complaint."

I sat back in my chair. This was going to be official. "What if I just pay her?" I said again.

Layton steepled his fingers and frowned at me. "You know that's the wrong thing to do."

"I know."

"Then what's making you hesitate?"

"I haven't told Trent," I said after a while.

"Ah," Layton murmured. "You think he'll take it badly?"

"No," I said instantly, and I knew I was right. "He won't care what I did before, but I don't want to be the one who fucks up this show he's making with things from my past."

"Okay, then I have another option."

That filled me with hope; any chance of some other way of dealing with this was a good thing. Right.

Layton opened a fat envelope; photos, papers and a CD slipped onto his desk.

"What is that?"

He pushed it all toward me, and I turned around the first of the photos. The contents were grainy, but it was clearly Marianna with two guys. I couldn't make out who the men were.

"She's done it before; you weren't some random guy she dated and tried to frame."

Weird how that news didn't shock me. Marianna and I had dated for maybe four weeks total, and the sex had been on from day one. She'd always pushed for a third, and hell, I'd been up for it.

"I was a mark."

Layton shuffled the papers and another photo, and handed them to me. "Her real name is Susan Kenton, US passport, and she's known to the police. This is the first time she's targeted hockey, but she's worked the West Coast and down in Dallas with the Cowboys."

So Marianna wasn't who she said she was. She wasn't French at all, and she was someone who used sex as a way to make money. I'd been conned, and somehow that shifted what I'd done. Of course I'd been in a threesome – a pretty hot one, to be fair – but at least the filming hadn't been done to expose that to the world; it had been done to get me to pay.

"Did the Cowboys pay?"

Layton pulled all the papers together. "This is where it gets interesting. She's pushed it too far now, and they've called in the cops. If you did the same, it wouldn't be something where it was your word against hers. It would be real."

And I'd have to tell Trent. Now instead of later.

"And the Railers can handle that?" I asked, rather than focusing on Trent.

Layton sat back in his seat, "If that's what you want to do, the team will find a way to manage any fallout."

When I left the arena, I drove back to my apartment, but didn't stop. Instead I headed east to Philly. If this was going to be public, I needed to tell Trent, and my parents, in that order.

He was on the ice, dressed head to toe in black, skating with a shorter version of himself. I couldn't see him properly from where I was standing, and I didn't make it obvious I was there, skulking at the back of the rink and waiting for the lesson to be over.

I should have known that he would spot me – he had this ability to see me even when I was hiding. He gestured for me to come down, and I did, every step feeling like an ax was about to fall.

When I reached him, the kisses helped with my nerves, but I clearly wasn't as into it as I thought I was – either that or Trent was crazy intuitive.

"What?" he asked, and stepped back. "What's wrong?"

"Can we talk?"

He went from bright, happy Trent to unsure in a second. Taking me by the hand, he led me away from the ice and down a corridor. He switched on lights and shut a door, and I realized we had somehow made it to his manager's office.

"You should sit down," I said, and encouraged him to his chair. But he pushed me away and stubbornly refused to sit.

"If we're done, then we're done," he said flatly, and crossed his arms over his chest. "Just tell me and leave."

"What? No."

I pulled him to me, and for a moment I felt back on track because he was in my arms. Then it hit me again what I needed to tell him. What if what I'd done, what Marianna had done, meant that the reality show was hit?

"It's me," I said. "I did something stupid, and there are photos of this threesome."

Trent eased himself away from me and resumed that position with his arms crossed over his chest, defensive, a little hunched. He looked like I'd kicked him, and I hurried with my explanation.

"The woman I was with videoed it and is looking for money to keep it private. Layton says she's done it to others, it wasn't just me, but I'm sorry it happened. Not sorry about the sex, but about being filmed, and it being out there potentially causing an issue for you."

"You cheated on me," Trent said, so very softly, his eyes bright and his posture beaten. "You lied to me, just like my stepdad."

I didn't understand what he meant. I hadn't cheated on him; I would never do anything to him that would cause the kind of pain he had on his face.

"No, shit, this was before I even met you."

He looked at me suspiciously, like he was weighing up the truth of what I was saying.

"I love you. I would never cheat on you, Trent. But I understand if this is too much, if I've fucked up." God, I sounded manic, like I was totally out of control in this, and Trent said nothing back.

The first thing I noticed was that Trent relaxed, his arms now loose at his sides, and he also held himself taller, almost to my chin still in his skates.

"You in a threesome," he began carefully. "We should so discuss that on camera. Viewers would love that."

"Huh?" I knew I was standing there like an idiot.

"Or maybe not. I'm guessing this is a police matter?"

"If I make it official, everyone will know."

Trent shrugged. "Everyone isn't important. I'm important." He said the last part with a smirk, and somehow I knew I had *my* Trent back.

"You can have my money," I blurted, "for the rink, if anything happens because I fucked up. Hell, you can have it all anyway."

He blinked at me, then he did that smile thing again, and I was lost. I wasn't sure who started the kiss first, but the mutually satisfying hand jobs with him still in skates was something I wouldn't forget in a hurry.

"I don't need your money," he said.

"But you'll take it if the rink is hit hard by any of this?"

He could have said no to that. He could have laughed it off, or taken every cent I owned, but he didn't.

"I'd do it for the kids," he said.

MY FIRST GAME BACK, against the physical Flyers, should have made me nervous, but it didn't. I was pumped from days before. As soon as they said I could start on the twenty-third, I was there, mentally and physically. I'd yet to hear anything official about the Marianna shit, but I'd given a statement, and Trent had been with me the entire time.

We had dinner in the early evening on the day before the game – a kind of meet-the-family thing, which was going okay. I refuse to say it was a perfect meet-up; Trent brought his *Lola*, and my parents had to deal with my flamboyant boyfriend and his equally colorful grandma dressed from head to toe in orange.

"So you a Railers fan?" *Lola* said, with as much contempt in her voice as she could muster.

"I'm a fan of whatever team my son plays for," Mom said, like she was daring *Lola* to say something back.

"So am I," Trent piped up, and squeezed my hand under the table.

But it didn't stop there, because *Lola* rounded on my dad, who I think was in shock. He'd long ago become used to his son having both boyfriends and girlfriends, but he'd never really met one like Trent before. He'd been polite, but had taken to looking at Trent when he thought Trent wasn't looking. I was beginning to feel a little uncomfortable.

"What about you?" *Lola* asked my dad, whose eyes widened at the direct question. I knew my dad's heart lay with Vancouver, and failing that any other Canadian team, but he was masterful at handling the people in my career.

"Flyers all the way," he lied.

Lola looked at him, then broke into a wide grin. "You good liar, Mr. Lehmann."

I brought my hand up to the surface of the table, with Trent's still grasped in mine, and joined in the laughter, feeling like nothing in my life could go wrong.

One day soon I would have to explain to Mom and Dad about Marianna, but by the time I did maybe it would be nothing more than a shitty memory. I had priorities in my life that weren't about scheming exes who wanted my money.

Dinner finished at eight and we separated, me back to my place without Trent, but not before I'd kissed him goodbye.

"See you tomorrow," he said, then waved at me from

the cab. I wanted to ask him to come home with me, but I needed sleep, and when I was with Trent? I didn't sleep.

When I got back to my place, as soon as the door shut on me and I was alone, what was happening the next day flooded me, overwhelmed me, and I had to sit down.

Tomorrow I would be dragging myself onto the ice, and I desperately wanted it to go well. I couldn't consider the possibility that some hard-ass would check me into the boards, hurt me, take me out. I had to stay focused. I was fast, I was fit, I was on the third line. I could do this.

"YOU CAN DO THIS," Ten said to me when he came back over the boards. He'd already said it to me twice before, but this time he was bright with the excitement of his first shift done and a shot on goal. It hadn't gone in, but that wasn't important. I could feel it in my bones that it was just a matter of time.

I looked up at where I knew Trent was sitting, right next to my parents. I'd got the tickets for them myself when they'd demanded to sit in with everyone else and not miles away in a box. I could see *Lola*, a bright orange dot in a sea of dusky blue.

I felt the tap on my shoulder, heard line change call.

And in a smooth movement, I was over the boards and into my first game in months.

FIFTEEN

Trent
___

"Hurry. We already miss anthem!"

Lola tugged on my arm, steering me through throngs of Railers fans. They all parted for us, but the sour looks were noted. Whether they were glaring at me in my spiffy duds or my grandmother in her Flyers paraphernalia, it was hard to say.

"Hey, why don't you go back to Philly?" some man carrying two beers shouted.

Guess that answered that.

"Why don't you go suck dirty eggs?!" my petite little grandmother fired back. "We beat your ass tonight! You see!"

"*Lola*, oh my gods, will you stop picking fights with the Railers fans?" I weaved around in front of her and purposely directed her away from the beer man and toward our seats.

"He started it," she snapped, and threw her chin up proudly. "I fight them all. Come get me, little man with big beer belly and puny dick!"

"*Lola!*" I could feel the heat rushing up my neck. "I

swear, if you get into a fight like you did last year at home, I am going to be so cross with you."

'Hey, last time that guy started it. He from Jersey." I showed a nice man in a vest our tickets as *Lola* rambled on about people from Trenton or some such thing. "Why he come over river anyway?"

"Maybe he was there to see his boyfriend play in his first game back after a horrible summer?"

"No, I don't think he has boyfriend or girlfriend. I think he has hand."

The fellow in the vest snickered.

"Don't laugh, it only encourages her," I muttered, and we descended into the sea of dusky blue jerseys. Wonderful. My grandmother was the only person in orange. We'd have beer on our heads before the first period was over.

My belly was a whirling mess. Dieter's parents were there, and even though they'd been nice last night, Dieter's dad certainly didn't give anything away. They hated me, I just knew it, and so I'd dampened my usual vibrant me down a few gigawatts. I'd just worn the jersey that Dieter had given me, with his name and number on the back, a pair of dark jeans, and some nice little moccasins with fleece inside. My eyeliner and gloss were minimal at best, and my hair was uncolored and gelled back from my face. I was boring. But boring is best when dealing with parents.

"See, I tell you we miss anthem."

"Sorry." I wiggled around a large man with a plate of nachos, then stopped at our row. "I know you love to sing the anthem, but I have no control over the accident by the capitol that made us late. There they are." My stomach spun. Dieter's parents glanced up. I wanted to run back to Philly. Instead I gave them a finger-wave.

"Stop worrying. They love you just like I do, babes." *Lola* shoved me, and I tripped over the feet of a woman sitting beside a thin black man. "Look, there my man!" *Lola* waved at her favorite player as he skated past.

"Excuse me." I stepped over their feet, gently pulled my grandmother along, and made my way to our seats. "Hello." I held out my hand to the lovely woman with Dieter's eyes. The man at her side gave me a long, odd look, but he finished it with a smile and shook my hand.

"Hey! You think you could sit down, sunshine?" a man behind us shouted.

"Trent, we're thrilled to watch this game with you," Mrs. Lehmann said after I dropped my ass into my seat.

Lola was still standing, arms over her head, chanting at the Flyers as they congregated at center ice.

"LET'S GO PHILLY! RAILERS ARE SILLY!" *Lola* roared at the top of her lungs.

Mrs. Lehmann giggled.

"I make up that cheer just for this game," *Lola* said, then sat down, her eyes sparkling.

"I'm sorry we're late. There was an accident that held us up for thirty minutes. I thought *Lola* would combust." I took off my dark blue coat and laid it over my lap.

Mr. Lehmann kept sneaking peeks at me around his wife. Probably he was trying to get his head wrapped around the idea that his son was in love with a man who wore more makeup than his wife. He'd had since last night to get used to it, but I knew it could take longer.

"It's fine. You're just in time for the first line change." Mrs. Lehmann pointed down at the ice.

Dieter had found us among the fans. His gaze touched mine. I shot to my feet and waved my arms over my head. A small smile tickled his mouth. My stars, that mouth. I had plans for that mouth – and other parts of his hot body – later. Booking hotel rooms for myself and *Lola* had been a brilliant move, if I did say so myself. She could snore away in her room and Dieter and I could fuck away in ours.

"Hey, buddy, sit down!" Irate Railers Man barked at me. I hurried to take my seat.

I sat on the edge of it for several minutes, trying to keep up with the action. It wasn't easy, and I'll confess to having little working knowledge of the game. I'd kept my distance from hockey players in the past. How ironic that I now was head-over-tasteful-heels in love with one.

"You watch your man in corners. He good in there. Fierce, hungry."

"Right, watch in the corners."

I did as *Lola* had said, and I could begin to see a sort of pattern to the way things ran. Mostly. Somewhat. I still didn't get why they kept stopping play for icing. Or how a person could be offside. That rule made no sense. But I enjoyed myself nonetheless. Dieter and the Railers looked good.

"Meh," *Lola* said when I mentioned that to her. "First game always bad. New lines, new players. They not gel until maybe ten games into season."

Showed what I knew. During the intermission, I climbed over my grandmother, visited the little boys' room, and brought us each a beer and a plate of nachos. By the time I got back to my seat, the second period was already underway.

"Dieter just pulled a penalty," Mrs. Lehmann informed me when I was in my seat.

"Oh no! What did he do?" I looked at the penalty box but he wasn't in it.

"Oh, he sneaky that man of yours!" *Lola* grumbled, then shoved a cheesy nacho into her mouth.

I sipped at my beer and watched the replay. *Oh, so pulling a penalty means...*

"I'm confused," I confessed to Mrs. Lehmann.

"He got the Philadelphia player to hook him."

"Oh, well yay!" I bounced up and down, but carefully so as not to spill my beer on my clothes. "And getting someone to hook you is good?"

"Yep, see now they're on the power play," Mrs. Lehmann explained. "That means they have a man up, since the other team is one man down. It gives them an advantage."

"THAT NO HOOK! YOU REF BLIND AS BAT!"

I winced at *Lola*'s angry shouting. The Railers players were talking among themselves before the face off. Tennant Rowe was out there, as was Dieter, which was exciting. I loved watching him play his game. I wondered if he liked to see me skate. I'd have to ask.

Things got pretty frantic then on the ice. The Railers swarmed around the Philadelphia net, shooting the puck at the harried Flyers goalie time and again. The Philadelphia defense seemed to be having a difficult time with the unit out there now. I could see why. All that talk about Tennant Rowe was accurate. He seemed to have a sixth sense about where the puck was going to be, and somehow he was always there.

"GAH! SOMEONE GET ROWE OUT OF CREASE!!" *Lola* was beside herself. The other people in the arena were thrilled.

Tennant passed the puck to Dieter, who was way back from the net. The men in bright orange turned to give my man their attention, and Dieter then took a shot that blistered past two Flyers, bounced off another, and somehow found the end of Tennant Rowe's stick. The puck did this funky wobbly thing as it sailed over the Flyers goalie and fell behind him and rolled to the back of the net. The East River Arena vibrated with cheers and an incredibly loud goal horn. Mrs. Lehmann, Mr. Lehmann, and I shot to our feet, clapping and yelling.

"Pah, lucky shot." *Lola* waved a fist at the replay of the Railers goal on the Jumbotron. "Dieter do good with assist," she conceded, then shouted something at the ref in Pilipino.

I was thrilled to see Dieter in a small knot on the ice, him and the other men in his unit slapping Tennant on his helmet. He looked so damn happy. And healthy. It made me feel ticklish inside seeing him doing what he loved so much.

By the end of the second, the Flyers had tied it up, but ended up losing after Tennant set up one of the other forwards, whose name escapes me, and the Railers got a goal. It was well after eleven when Dieter was freed from the dressing room and after-game press talks. His parents and I lingered around outside the arena, making small talk, while *Lola* sat in my new sassy yellow Prius eating a soft pretzel while listening to the radio.

I thought he would greet his parents first, but he walked right up to me. He looked incredible. There's just something about a man in a suit. His hair was damp from his post-game shower, and his eyes smoldered like fiery emeralds. His hand went to the back of my neck and he pressed his lips to mine. The kiss was kind of stiff, since his parents were right there. He released my neck, then took my hand before turning to talk to his folks. His mom, who was adorable – and a figure skater, so of course she was precious – seemed fine with all the man love. His dad... well, he wasn't curt or anything, but you could tell he was working through his stuff. And that was cool. I knew I was a shock to the system for some people.

"I was thinking we could get together in the morning for breakfast," Dieter quickly tossed out when his mother asked about going for drinks. "I'm sure Trent's grandmother is exhausted. She's really old."

Lola could be heard singing along with Bon Jovi about bad medicine.

"Yeah, she's done in," I said, and averted my gaze.

The lie was feeble, but Mrs. Lehmann bought it. Or maybe she just knew we wanted time alone. It *had* been a couple of weeks for us; my rink time was beginning to gobble up my personal time. But money was money, and since I wasn't sure if I'd get paid for the TV show or not since I'd acted up outside the prison, I needed every damn dime I could get.

"Breakfast would be fab!" I added.

"Okay, breakfast it is." Mrs. Lehmann kissed her son.

Dieter and his father shook hands. Talk was made about assists and good checking as we tried to wiggle free.

Ten minutes later, we'd broken away and were on our way to the hotel. It was a nice one that overlooked the river. I got *Lola* into her room, then ran down the hall to mine, my overnight bag thumping on my back. Dieter lingered just outside my door, his hands in his pockets. The sexual tension was so thick in the corridor you could feel it on your skin like fog on a cool night.

I swiped my key card and stepped inside. Dieter followed, shut the door, and flicked on a light. A small lamp on a long dresser flared to life. I dropped my bag to the floor, turned to look at Dieter, and began taking off my clothes. He did the same. His personal bag was flung onto a plump chair in the corner and then he began undressing. Tie first, then jacket, dress shirt and undershirt, shoes, socks, belt, trousers and then his sexy little briefs. By the time his cock was in view, I already had my dick in hand, stroking it root to tip.

"Come here," I said, and he did, without a moment's

hesitation. His fingers went around mine, tightening the grip on my cock. Tremors of pleasure ran through me. My gaze settled on that mouth. Time to put it to use. "I want you to drop to your knees and suck on me for a while. Then you need to get on that bed and offer that sweet ass to me."

He grunted, stole a deep kiss, then went to his knees.

"You okay down there?" I asked as the lust cloud lifted for just a second. Maybe a man who'd just rehabbed from knee surgery shouldn't be kneeling. I was a terrible boyfriend.

"Stop worrying and enjoy."

He licked a hot line up and down my cock, then rolled his tongue over the head, eagerly lapping up the precum coating it. My eyes drifted shut. Dieter sucked me down, taking me as deeply as he could. I rolled my hips, shoved my fingers into his damp hair, and pumped in and out of his mouth. His eyes stayed locked with mine. It was beautiful and dirty and so fucking erotic I had to pull out several times to stall the impending orgasm.

"You want me on the bed now?" he asked during one of those stops.

I nodded as I battled to calm my breathing. He got up with ease, licked at my mouth, then crawled over the bed, his ass high and proud. The sight of that tight hole and his dangling balls had me falling over myself to find the lube and condoms in my overnight bag.

"Trent, hurry up. I need you to fuck me."

"No rush," I replied as I rolled the condom down over me.

One knee to the bed, then the other. The weight of the hockey player offering himself so delectably to me made the mattress dip deeply in the middle. He gyrated his hips when my cock brushed his ass, and a long, low moan of desire rumbled out of him.

"Yes, fucking rush. I need you in me," he huffed as he went to his elbows.

Pillows slid to the floor. I flipped open the lube. He groaned at the sound. Fingers slick as my cock, I pushed two into him. The big man arched back, his spine bowed like a Halloween cat. I toyed with his ass for a bit, working the lube into him, pressing on his prostate, enjoying the sight and sound of this fingering.

"Trent, for fuck's sake, man!"

"You really want to be fucked, don't you?" I slid my fingers out and pressed myself to him, my cock slipping up between his taut cheeks. "Tell me how badly you want to be fucked."

"Fuck, Trent, I need you so bad," he said, his voice low and smoky. I ran my fingers up his sides. He shuddered, his skin rising with gooseflesh. "Fuck me – do it now before I come all over my hand."

Taking myself in hand, I pressed the head of my cock into him. There was resistance at first, and then his inner muscles relaxed and I pushed in deeper and deeper and deeper still. Dieter grabbed the back of his head with both hands when I flicked my hips, a keen of pleasure filling the overly warm hotel room.

"Jesus, Trent…"

"I know," I gasped. The sheer pleasure of being joined with him was beyond description, so I didn't try to form words to speak. My body spoke for me. I gave it free rein to do so.

The rhythm we quickly fell into was wild, fast, manic. Dieter came as I rocked in and out of him, his hands still locked behind his head. The clench of him around me pushed me over the edge. I thrust hard, pulling him back onto me, and tumbled off the cliff.

"Oh…shit…oh," the man under me coughed, his strong legs the only thing keeping us from tumbling to the bed. My spine and all the other bones in my body were now goop. Cock kicking inside him, I bowed down over his back and bit down on his shoulder. "Shit…baby…yeah," he crooned heatedly. My cock slid out and I fell on top of him then slithered off, shivering from the orgasm still gripping me.

"Ah, lord above," I whispered, grabbing my cock, and giving it a slow, final stroke.

Dieter went to his belly amid the tousled blankets and sheets. "Oh fuck, I made a mess," he complained, but didn't move. "Can we call housekeeping at midnight for clean sheets?" The covers muffled his voice.

"I doubt it."

He rolled toward me, his weight pinning me to the bed as he battled to get the wet spot covered with one of the four blankets hotels always put on beds.

"You're heavy," I said, then wiggled free of the gorilla on top of me.

He chuckled. "You love it. You get hot about how I can toss you around in bed, don't deny it."

I didn't. I could not lie. I loved that he was so big and I was so small.

"True, it's all true."

He moved me toward him, pulling me close to his side then pressing me into the bed and kissing me so tenderly I wanted to weep.

"I love you, Trent."

"I love you too."

His eyes were damp now. "I mean it. You stood by me through some awful shit."

"I'm a stander, what can I say?" I chased his lips, eager for more of his kisses.

"Say you'll keep standing by me." He drew back to stare into my eyes.

"Always, babes, always."

I lifted my head from the rumpled sheets. This time I managed to catch a kiss or two or twenty.

SIXTEEN

Dieter

W hen the call came, I'd been expecting it. Layton had warned me that he'd been talking to his counterpart down in Dallas, and that the net was closing on Marianna, or Susan Kenton – I didn't know what to call her in my head anymore. She was a serial blackmailer, but I'd been with her for a month; how the hell had I let myself get into that situation? I didn't recall a specific time when I'd thought she was fake; I just knew that toward the end of *us* she had become very interested in the possibility of a new contract with the Railers.

I'd bet she'd been expecting the kind of money the big guys got; my less-than-a-million payout probably seemed puny to her, but still she'd gone after it.

"You okay?"

Connor leaned on the same wall as me, bumping elbows. He was clearly there as representation, or support, something confirmed when Toly arrived as well. My captain *and* the player rep? Maybe I should have called my brand-new agent for her to be in the room as well.

"I'm good," I said, shuffling from foot to foot, really

wanting to get inside Layton's office to find out what was going on.

"It's been some season," he said dryly. "What with Ten and Jared, and now you and your blackmail."

"And sleeping with the pretty-boy figure skater," Toly said with an added chuckle. "I like your pretty-boy."

I shot the Russian a quick look. I could never tell whether he was joking or not; he had one of those faces that gave nothing away.

Connor cleared his throat dramatically, and Toly laughed even louder. "He is very good on his skates," Toly pointed out. "That is all."

Connor cursed under his breath and Toly gave something back, the two of them bickering and teasing, and it flowed over me with familiar warmth.

I loved it there. I never wanted to be traded, I wanted to play out my years there. Of course, that wouldn't happen. I'd do well there, or I wouldn't. I'd stay, or I'd get traded. Whatever happened, I was there right now, and coming off last night's win against Vancouver and the gloating rights that gave me over Dad, I was in a good place.

I wasn't even that nervous about this meeting.

Or at least not as nervous as I could have been.

"Did you hear that?" Connor said, loud enough to break through my internal ramblings.

"What?"

"'Toly is wearing a purple-and-green suit to the wedding." He was clearly shocked by this, but then he would be. He was the best-dressed guy on the team by far, with his designer suits and his neat beard. Quite a few sports magazines had had his face on the cover, alongside one GQ spread where even I'd found myself disappointed he was straight.

The wedding was the occasion of the Railers' year, between our marketing lady, Emma, and her fiancé Paul. We'd all been invited.

I fist-bumped Toly. "Trent was muttering something about scarlet."

Connor rolled his eyes.

I opened my mouth to tell them about my dark navy suit and plain shirt, but Layton's door opened.

I gestured for Connor and Toly to go in first, and was just about to step in myself when a loud voice came from behind me.

"Am I too late?"

Gayle, Trent's agent and now my agent, stood there looking like she'd run up all five flights of stairs.

"I wasn't expecting you," I offered lamely.

"Trent said you had a meeting. You should start telling me these things, idiot."

She swatted my arm and went into the meeting, and I followed, cowed by her chastisement and also by the mood of the room. Everyone looked so serious.

"What?" I said, and looked right at Layton, who was standing behind his desk.

"She pleaded guilty," he said in one simple sentence, no exaggeration or explanation. I was lost for what to say.

"What does that mean?" Connor asked, vocalizing what I wanted to say but couldn't.

"It's over. Some statements, but she's plea-bargaining, and we could get past this without your name attached to it legally."

"That won't stop it from being made public," Gayle said. I was thankful for her and Connor's presence.

"No, it won't, but there will be no video release, no stills, and no money paid, so I think we can call this a win."

Even thirty minutes later, out on the ice, running drills,

I was still dazed – so much so that I skated into the net, narrowly missing a very irritable Stan. He pushed me forcefully away from his crease, causing me to fall, then stood over me telling me off in a mess of broken English and angry Russian. I just lay there and took it, but when he stopped talking, obviously wanting me to comment, I got up and hugged the big guy. After a while he patted my back.

We parted, and I skated away, snowing the guys waiting at the other end.

"What was that about?" Ten asked, inclining his head at Stan.

I shrugged. "I skated too near him, he didn't like it, he said some shit none of which I understood, and we hugged it out."

Practice was skills and stretches, and afterward lunch at a local bar. Life with my teammates and friends was good.

But I missed Trent.

"HEAVENS ABOVE, who taught you to fix a tie?" Trent asked. He attempted to tie it again for me, but the height difference was kind of an awkward mess of me stooping and him on tiptoes. In the end, he cursed under his breath and clambered up on the coffee table, putting his height a little above mine. That way he could concentrate on getting my sapphire-blue tie as perfect as he wanted it.

"You know I've been doing my own ties for years now," I said. Not that I minded that he was so close to me, fiddling with my clothes. In fact, I might well have made today's effort a little messy just so he would come to my rescue.

This close, I could see the warmth of the brown in his eyes, the sweep of color on his lids, and the smudge of liner. He'd put gloss on his lips – this was the third time, because I kept kissing it off him. I couldn't help it; his lips all slick like that were enticing. He straightened the tie a little, then tutted just before I kissed him again.

"Stop that," he said, but there was no heat in his words and he deepened the kiss. I lifted him, and he wrapped his legs around me.

"We should kiss some more," I demanded, and attempted to do so. He avoided my kiss and wriggled free of my hold.

"We'll be late," he said, checking his lips in the mirror and applying more gloss. I watched him the same way I did every time he did that, and caught a glimpse of the shine on my own lips. I wasn't quite ready for a public appearance with gloss, and wiped at the slick of it with a tissue, but it wouldn't be long before I had my lips on his again.

When we arrived, I spotted Toly immediately in his purple-and-green suit. He looked good, and of course Connor was front and center looking like the GQ model he was. Ten and Jared were hand in hand, and Layton stood so close to Adler it wouldn't be long before that secret was out.

As for me, I took Trent's hand and tugged him toward the group. Trent fit in there, despite his scarlet suit, his dark hair with streaks of red, and his makeup. He was a skater – ice was his mistress, the same way as it was for all of us.

The wedding was beautiful, as weddings are, and afterward it was back to Connor's place for a surprise. He wouldn't tell us what it was, but it was something that Trent had organized, so God knew what I expected.

We were all handed champagne – just the tiniest of glasses, because Connor was way past responsible at all times – and then he instructed us to take a seat in his home cinema room. Yep, he was *that* player, with the cinema seating and the large screen, and he'd even set up extra chairs; there were hockey players sprawled everywhere. I was lucky enough to get one of the cinema seats, and Trent decided to sit on my lap.

Since we'd arrived, he'd been a little twitchy, and I held him close; maybe someone had said something, or he was worried about whatever was happening here.

"What is this?"

"They'll have made me a figure of fun," he whispered to me, his voice tight with emotion. "Please don't be too embarrassed."

"I don't understand," I said, but I didn't get to say anything else, because Connor turned the lights off and took a chair.

"Ready?" he asked, and we all nodded, and then in unison said yes, because hockey players aren't stupid – we'd all come to the same conclusion that it was dark and no one could see our nods.

The screen lit up, a flashy image in sparkling diamonds that segued to ice in the sun, then moved on to a rink.

"This winter," the announcer said in a typical movie voice, "join Trenton Lawrence, Olympic figure skater, as he attempts to corral a rink of hockey players…"

Oh, it's the show, or at least some kind of trailer.

Trent's face appeared, and he was smiling, and then the image zoomed out to us, the big hulking hockey players that dwarfed him. We were standing in a semi-circle, like we'd been placed; I recalled they'd stood me to one side to balance Stan, or something like that. That single image was so telling. How was this itty-bitty figure skater going to handle us?

The presenter said some other stuff. I wasn't listening – I was holding Trent tight and hoping to hell this went well.

The picture disappeared into diamonds again, and this time we had Stan on the screen, jumping, arms extended, in full goalie gear, ending in a cartwheel.

Over the top, Trent's voice. "Only by learning the basics can we work with the strength…"

The camera had caught Stan tumbling to the floor, then moved right to Ten, who barreled into him mid-spin. I couldn't help smiling, and I heard Stan's Russian and Ten's snort of laughter in the room.

They weren't poking fun at Trent; in fact it was the complete opposite.

The film showed other falls, then moved on to some of the things the guys had learned, brief glimpses of before and after stats.

"So join Trent and his friends for a Christmas launch of the new reality show…"

I tuned out again, seeking Trent's lips with my own and kissing him.

Then I said what I thought he needed to hear. "I couldn't be prouder."

Epilogue

TRENT

"Are we sure this is cool?" Dieter asked, his new Flyers jersey looking more than a bit odd on him. The black hockey skates dangling off his broad shoulder looked fitting.

"It's my rink. If we want to sneak in at midnight, we can."

"Yeah, okay. Can I take this off now?" He plucked at the vibrant orange jersey, lifting the shoulder a bit then letting it drop. You could just see the flash of the brown sweater he'd worn to dinner around the loose collar of the jersey. "I mean, I appreciate your grandmother buying it for me for my birthday and all, but...it feels weird."

"Sure, you can take it off." I snickered while unlocking the front door of Rainbow Skate. We hurried inside and I locked the door behind us.

He yanked the sweater – I'd learned that was what hockey players called jerseys – over his head, leaving his hair twisted and standing up. I reached up to flatten it down.

"I wish we had more time together," I sighed as the thick mass just stood back up.

"I told you that once we were into the season things would be tight, babe."

"I know, I know." I pushed my hand through his hair, not to tidy it, just to feel it slipping over my fingertips. "I'd consider moving my coaching business to Harrisburg, but my kids couldn't make the move."

"It'll work out. It's only two hours one way. Like today, right? I just get up early tomorrow and I'm back at the barn in time for morning skate."

"Of course, I know. It's just…the nights alone are hard."

"That's the life of a hockey wife," he teased, then danced out of reach of my swat to his ass.

"I'd make a *divine* hockey spouse."

"Yeah, you would. Come on, let's do some ice time."

He latched onto my wrist, pulling me to the ice area. We sat down and began lacing up skates. His were twice the size of mine. I pointed that out and got a neck-nibble for stroking his ego a bit.

"So, I see your mom looks happier. Are you and Clay talking yet?"

I frowned down at my laces.

"We're not talking, actually." I exhaled and sat back, leaving my laces dangling. "It's more like…" I wasn't sure how to explain it. I thumbed a blue strand of hair from my face. "Well, it's more like we're not actually talking, but we're not actually not."

"That made no sense at all," he stated flatly.

"I know. It's still a massive problem for me. I keep trying to work it out, you know, in counseling and talking about it with Mom and *Lola*, but I can't seem to get past the betrayal. Please don't ever cheat on me or lie to me. I can take quite a lot, but…"

"Hey, look at me." He took my chin and turned my head. I loved his eyes. "First off, who the hell else would want me? Ex-addicts aren't high on most people's turn-on list."

I shot him a look of disgust, but he was teasing me.

"Joking aside, there is no other man who could ever take your place. Have you looked in the mirror lately?"

"I *am* rather stunning, aren't I?" I teased back, and the weight of my relationship with Clay – such as it was – lifted a bit. "I'm not sure I can skate. I ate too much birthday dinner," I moaned, and rubbed my protruding belly after lacing up.

Dieter placed his hand over mine. "You're as flat as a board. Sexy, too." He let his hand slither down toward my crotch. I swatted his wandering fingers away.

"Nope, no petting until we skate. This is my present to you. Well," I stood up, popped out a hip and gave him a smoky look, "it's *one* of my presents. The other involves lube and a butt plug I bought for you. Oops. Guess *that* cat is out of its bag!"

"Shit, I have a half chub just thinking about that." He chuckled, pushed to his feet, and followed me over the thick matting to the sound system.

"I had the CD I burned on top," I sighed as I began pawing through soundtracks for *Frozen*, *Beauty and the Beast*, and *Mary Poppins*. "The kids do love their Disney."

"How's Scotty doing? She okay with school and all?" He stepped behind me, his breath moist and warm on the back of my neck.

"She's doing well. Such a brave thing. Ah! Here it is."

I waved the CD over my head, then slid it into the old stereo. Now that I'd gotten the first of my checks from the

TV show as well as my payment from the Railers, I had plans to upgrade things around here. I'd already paid off the mortgage on my mother's house. The taxes had been paid as well, on both properties. The check to the bank was in the mail for Rainbow Skate. I could breathe again.

"Good. She's a nice kid."

"Yes, she is. They're all wonderful students."

We took off our skate guards and stepped onto the ice, his fingers laced with mine.

"You look happy," he said, then took off, pulling me behind him as we slowly made a lap around the ice.

"I am. Deliriously so." I turned to face him, skating in reverse so I could watch the play of emotions run over his expressive face. "You have so much to do with my happiness level. I thought I'd lost all my happy. Then you skated into my world."

"And turned it right into a shitfest." His brows tangled a bit as we did a few easy crossovers.

"No, you did not." He spun me around, then pulled me back, pressing me against his chest as "Wonderwall" by Oasis began to fill the rink. "It was already a shitfest. You gave me a reason to battle out of the mess. We were fated. Like Romeo and Juliet, only minus the poison and cursing in Italian."

His head dropped, his brow resting on mine, our skates gliding over the fresh ice, his arms around me.

"You saved me. You know that, right?"

A livelier song began, "Electric Love", one that I'd toyed with skating to at one time. But that had been a lifetime ago. Now the medals and the flowers falling to the ice didn't seem as important as seeing Scotty smile after nailing a single salchow. And the accolades and fan adoration paled to being with this man on the nights we could wrangle couple time.

"*You* saved you," I reminded him, leaning back to allow him to swing me out. His grip was so strong, sure, steady. When I was upright, Dieter lifted me over his head. I rolled down to his shoulder a moment later, my arms looping around his neck, my skates barely touching the ice.

"Okay, but I had lots of support." He pressed a kiss to my chin as I slithered down the front of him.

"You'd make a very solid skating partner," I told him, my fingers playing with the soft hairs on the nape of his neck.

"Is that the only kind of solid partner you think I could be?" His lips trailed up from my chin to my lips, where he nibbled and licked for the length of an entire song. I let him lead us around the rink, his stride powerful and sure, mine light and steady.

"Goose," I purred between soft, sweet kisses. "I know you'll make a wonderful bowling partner."

Dieter snorted, our feet moving in perfect tandem with nary a trip or stumble. "You're not going to just say it, are you?"

"Doubtful. I like to play the minx," I confessed, darting away from him to build up enough speed that I could drop down to sail across the ice on my side, one leg tucked behind me and the other straight. It was quite the dramatic move, and one that had won me more than a few medals and championships.

Dieter skated over to where I was lying on the ice, my eyes closed, and my form perfect.

"The Canadian/German judge gives that move a perfect ten."

I cracked an eye open. "The Canadian/German judge is biased, but the American/Pilipino skater is okay with that."

He offered me his hand. I slipped mine into his and

was pulled to my skates and into his embrace. I traced his strong jaw with my cold fingers. His green-and-amber eyes began to smolder. We hadn't been on the ice long.

"You'll be an amazing life partner. That is if you want to spend the rest of your life with me?" I peeked through my eyelashes. "I'm known to be a little bratty and just a bit flamboyant."

"Just a bit, huh?" He thumbed my lower lip, smearing the pink gloss that he adored so much.

I nodded, then batted my darkened lashes.

"I love bratty, flamboyant men."

"Then we're a solid pair, aren't we?"

"We are now."

THE END

Poke Check (Harrisburg Railers Hockey #4)

One scorching summer in each other's arms could never be enough.

Stanislav "Stan" Lyamin is happy playing for the Railers. The towering goalie is well-loved, respected, and making a home for himself even though that home only contains him, his cat, and his growing Pokémon trading card collection. Stan prefers it that way. He'd given his heart to a man last summer in a secret affair, and that man walked away, leaving Stan shattered.

Now Erik is back in his life, and he has the same tumultuous effect he had on Stan's heart as before. This time it's not just a kissable mouth and sweet blond curls that Erik has brought to Harrisburg, there's a soon-to-be ex-wife and a precious baby. Despite the vow Stan made to hate Erik forever, he's now finding it harder and harder to turn away.

Erik Gunnarsson's dream had always been to play in the NHL; he just never imagined he'd land a contract with the Railers. Who would have thought that fate would put him on the same team as Stanislav Lyamin; the man whose heart he'd callously broken? Secrets and lies had defined their summer relationship, and the choice that Erik made to end it all haunts him still. In the middle of a messy divorce and with a baby in tow, Erik finds himself back in Stan's life. Now all he has to do is be the best dad he can be, prove to the team that he deserves the chance to stay on the roster and try his hardest to get Stan to forgive him. Is it possible to persuade a man who hates you to give love a second chance?

Harrisburg Railers

Owatonna U Hockey

Arizona Raptors

Boston Rebels

LA Storm

Chesterford Coyotes - Young Adult

Free Reads

Please note - in all of these free stories, there will be some spoilers for the main series books.

Railers Short Stories

Volume 1 | Volume 2

LA Storm

Sparkle

The Colts - AHL Short Stories

Pucks & Percentages

Breakaway

Making the Save

Standalone

Waiting for Christmas

When hockey wunderkind Tennant Rowe meets his new coach, he knows he's in trouble. Jared Madsen is nine years older than Tennant, impossibly attractive, and — worst of all — his brother's off-limits best friend. Is their chemistry worth the risk?

Changing Lines (Railers 1)

Can Tennant show Jared that age is just a number, and that love is all that matters?

The Rowe Brothers are famous hockey hotshots, but as the youngest of the trio, Tennant has always had to play against his brothers' reputations. To get out of their shadows, and against their advice, he accepts a trade to the Harrisburg Railers, where he runs into Jared Madsen. Mads is an old family friend and his brother's one-time teammate. Mads is Tennant's new coach. And Mads is the sexiest thing he's ever laid eyes on.

Jared Madsen's hockey career was cut short by a fault in his heart, but coaching keeps him close to the game. When Ten is traded to the team, his carefully organized world is thrown into chaos. Nine years his junior and his best friend's brother, he knows Ten is strictly off-limits, but as soon as he sees Ten's moves, on and off the ice, he knows that his heart could get him into trouble again.

Changing Lines

Harrisburg Railers (Hockey Romance)

1. Changing Lines
2. First Season
3. Deep Edge
4. Poke Check
5. Last Defense
6. Goal Line
7. Neutral Zone
8. Hat Trick
9. Save The Date
10. Baby Makes Three
11. Rivals
12. Perfect Gifts
13. Family First

Meet the men of Owatonna University's hockey team

Ryker (Owatonna U, 1)

Ryker

Ryker is hockey royalty, Jacob is a poor country boy. Can two vastly different people find common ground and become the men they want to be?

Ryker comes from a long line of championship-winning hockey players. Playing college hockey to develop his game is his only focus, and nothing will stand in the way of him working to become the best player. He has no room for relationships, people who point out his flaws, or anyone who calls him on his dreams. He certainly has no place for love, and meeting Jacob is nothing but a useful distraction on the side. After all trying to get his Owatonna Eagles teammate into bed is less work and more play. When tragedy rocks his family, his charmed life crumbles, and the only person he can turn to is the same one who claims to hate him.

Jacob Benson has only known hard work and stifling conservative values his whole life. Born and raised in the small rural community of Eden Crossing, Minnesota, he's the only son of a hard-working but struggling dairy farming family. Jacob is using his skills in hockey to finance his way to an agricultural science degree. These four years at Owatonna U. will probably be the only time he has to enjoy life, gain acceptance about his sexuality, and live openly before his inevitable return to the farm. Running into a pretty rich boy like Ryker Madsen is putting a damper on his enjoyment of life away from home. Ryker's flip, conceited, carefree attitude grates on Jacob's every nerve. So why, if Ryker is everything he dislikes, does he want nothing more than to explore the sinful dreams that his annoying teammate stars in every night?

Ryker

Owatonna U Hockey (Hockey Romance)

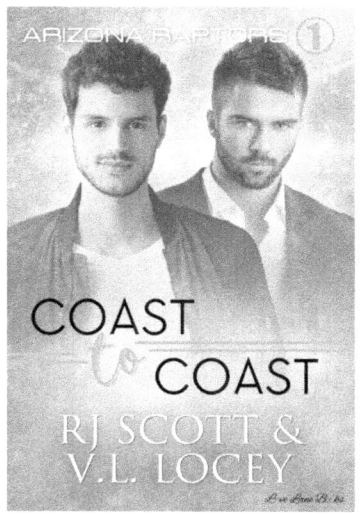

Coast to Coast (Arizona Raptors 1)

Coast To Coast

When opposites attract, this bottom-of-the-league team will never be the same again.

A stipulation in his father's will forces Mark back into the arms of a family that disowned him and leaves him one-third owner of a hockey team facing financial ruin. He doesn't even watch hockey, let alone like it, and wants nothing more than to head back to New York. Then there's the new coach, a stubborn, opinionated, irritating man with superiority issues and questionable music taste. Butting heads with Rowen becomes the new normal, but it comes with passionate debate and an all-consuming lust.

Challenged to rebuild one of the worst teams in the league into a future cup contender, Rowen can't pass up the opportunity. Never in his twenty years of hockey has he ever seen a team managed so badly or coached players overflowing with resentment and bigotry. Yet there's something about this team and this city that compels him to roll up his sleeves and start dismantling. If only Mark, one of three siblings who now own the Raptors, wasn't so damned rock-headed yet so damned appealing his job might be easier. It doesn't look like either is willing to give in, but one night in a dark, desert hotel changes everything.

Coast To Coast

Arizona Raptors (Hockey Romance)

1. Coast To Coast
2. Across the Pond
3. Shadow and Light
4. Sugar and Ice
5. School and Rock

Top Shelf (Boston Rebels 1)

Acting on the attraction to his best friend's brother has always been off the table for Xander until a passionate hookup with Mason at a beach resort begins a love affair that burns long after summer ends.

Mason specializes in assisting same-sex couples on their journey to becoming parents and fighting every rule that blocks his way in the stuck-in-the-past agency that hired him. Living in his brother's pool house is rent-free, and every cent he earns he saves for his dream—that one day he'd have his own company helping others. The downside is that he has to see his annoying brother every day, the upside is that his brother's teammates from the Boston Rebels make regular visits. The eye candy that passes Mason's window is almost enough to make him consider dating a hockey player, but not just any player though. Ever since Xander —his brother's childhood friend—came out as gay at a press conference, Mason's puppy love has turned into a burning attraction he can no longer ignore.

Hockey has been one of Xander's main focuses since he was old enough to balance on skates. Well, hockey and Mason Kingsley, but Mason was always unattainable. Now that he's about to see thirty candles on his birthday cake and is no longer hiding the fact he's gay, he's ready to find a soul mate to make his life complete. A summer vacation is just what he needs to have time to think, but when the Boston Rebels arriving in paradise with Mason in tow, thinking is the last thing he needs. One torrid night under a balmy moon and rules about not messing with his best friend's brother vanish on a warm, tropical breeze.

Summer romances don't generally last past Labor Day, but with the new season about to begin Xander and Mason are going to have to face the world and decide if their love is real enough to withstand everything.

Boston Rebels

Lost In Boston (Free Prequel Novella)

1. Top Shelf
2. Back Check
3. Snowed
4. Royal Lines
5. Blade
6. Rental

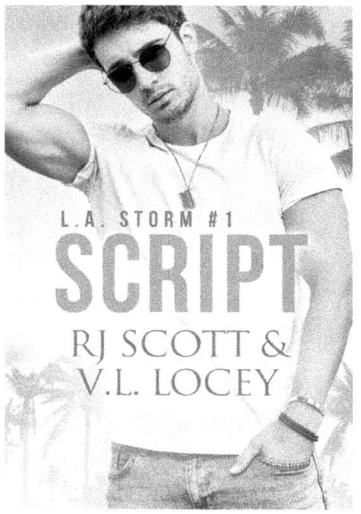

Script (LA Storm, 1)

Script

Hollywood A-lister Finn might be Canadian, but he needs Cameron to show him how to hockey.

Actor Finn Kerrigan is at a crossroads. After growing up a soap star, then starring in a hugely successful trilogy of action movies, he's finally given the chance to read a heartfelt and passionate script that could change his life forever. The role would be enough for people to see him as a serious actor, and maybe even win him an award or two (and no, a golden raspberry award for his action movies doesn't count). Once established as a serious actor he's sure he can come out of the closet and finally live his truth. When he lies to get the part of a hockey player on a struggling team, he suddenly has nowhere to hide. He might be Canadian, but the last time he skated he was ten, and no, he doesn't have hockey in his blood. With only a month until filming starts, he about to be exposed, but partnered with a player who's supposed to be giving him tips, he doesn't realize how many of his secrets will come to light. Falling in lust, one heated kiss at a time, is inevitable, but giving Cameron up at the end of the shoot could break his heart.

Cameron Chavkin is the face of the LA Storm. And the body, and the hair, and the smile. He's at the prime of his career, men and women want to be with him, and he's skating better than he ever has before. His house sits next to a famous rock star's mansion, his garage is filled with expensive cars, and he's even been asked to mentor a once-famous actor in a new hockey movie. Life is pretty sweet. Until the bad boy of hockey meets Finn, a man on the edge with more secrets than Cameron has endorsements. Knowing better than to get involved, Cameron is swept up despite himself, and when it's time to say goodbye to the Storm's most eligible bachelor is finding it hard to follow the script.

Script

~

LA Storm

Off The Ice (Chesterford Coyotes, 1)

Off The Ice

A coming-of-age love story with high school, hockey rivalry, friendship, family, and coming out.

Soren's life changes in an instant when he and his younger brother are adopted by hockey royalty. Making sense of his new life is hard enough, but when he's enrolled in a private school it means facing a whole new set of problems. Navigating friendship, family, and hockey is one thing, but being attracted to the boy who vexes him is a whole new thing.

Felix has a reputation to protect. He's the kid who seems to have everything but looks can be deceiving. Spinning lies about his perfect life, he's created a fantasy world that even he has started to believe. Only, it's not long before everything crumbles, all of his pretty lies are revealed, and only his closest rival sees through his pain and stands by him.

Fighting is easy, friendship is hard, but love is everything.

Off The Ice

Chesterford Coyotes

1. Off The Ice
2. On Thin Ice
3. *Dance on Ice*

Also By RJ Scott

For a full list of ebooks and links please scan the code above or visit rjscott.co.uk/rjbooks

Meet RJ Scott

RJ discovered romance in books at a very young age and realized that if there wasn't romance on the page, she could create it in her head. With over one hundred and fifty books published, she is a full time author of gay romance.

She lives and works out of her home in the beautiful English countryside, spends her spare time reading, watching films, and enjoying time with her family.

The last time she had a week's break from writing she didn't like it one little bit and has yet to meet a box of chocolates she couldn't defeat.

www.rjscott.co.uk | rj@rjscott.co.uk

NEWSLETTER - rjscott.co.uk/rjnews

facebook.com/author.rjscott

x.com/Rjscott_author

instagram.com/rjscott_author

amazon.com/author/rj-scott

bookbub.com/authors/rj-scott

goodreads.com/rjscott

pinterest.com/rjscottauthor

Also By VL Locey

For a full list of ebooks and links please scan the code above or
visit vllocey.com/stories-from-vl-locey

Meet V.L. Locey

V.L. Locey loves worn jeans, yoga, belly laughs, walking, reading and writing lusty tales, Greek mythology, the New York Rangers, comic books, and coffee.

(Not necessarily in that order.)

She shares her life with her husband, her daughter, one dog, two cats, a flock of assorted domestic fowl, and two Jersey steers.

When not writing spicy romances, she enjoys spending her day with her menagerie in the rolling hills of Pennsylvania with a cup of fresh java in hand.

vllocey.com
vicki@vllocey.com

Newsletter - vllocey.com/newsletter

facebook.com/V.L.Locey

x.com/vllocey

instagram.com/vl_locey

bookbub.com/authors/v-l-locey

goodreads.com/vllocey

pinterest.com/vllocey